HUDSONVILLE
WHAT LIES BENEATH

A Young Adult
Urban Fantasy

I0601803

Stewart Chisham

Culicidae Press, LLC
PO Box 5069
Madison, WI 53705-5069
culicidaepress.com
editor@culicidaepress.com

Madison | Berlin | Lemgo

ISBN: 978-1-68315-149-4

Our books may be purchased in bulk for promotional, educational
or business use. Please contact your local bookseller or the
Culicidae Press Sales Department at +1-352-215-7558
or by email at sales@culicidaepress.com

culicidaepress.bsky.social – facebook.com/culicidaepress
threads.net/@culicidaepress – instagram.com/culicidaepress
x.com/culicidaepress

Design by polytekton © 2025
Cover art by Beatriz Rebollo Art © 2025

DEDICATION

To my nephews Franco and Louie Lars

TABLE OF CONTENTS

PROLOGUE

August 2014

"Give it to me! Hurry!"

The downpour came, thunder cracking up above. They stood in a blasted forest clearing, surrounded by the clashing of weapons and shouting of men.

Martin's hand went to his coat pocket, feeling the weight of the heirloom within. His fingers glossed the rough gem in its center, the cold engravings pressed themselves into his palm. His hound-dog eyes sagged. There was his son, a mass of fur writhing underneath the heel of his fellow beast. There was no hope for a cure, no hope to be saved from this fate.

The old man stilled as Talia continued to beg for the object. Her angry pleas were all but drowned out by the rain.

"Now, Kessler!" Talia said, stepping toward him, impatient. The old man stepped back.

"I...I can't," Martin said quietly. The woman's scarred visage contorted.

"What do you mean you can't? This is what we came here for!"

Martin took another step back. "Not this."

"You can see it, can't you? That...*thing* is no longer your son. Martin. Give me the heirloom and I can end his suffering. It would be mercy."

The old man's grip tightened.

"You're wrong. My boy's still in there. He might be *different* now, but he's still my Andy."

"Do not be a fool. Your love for him cannot *blind* you. Look at him. That beast will tear you apart without a second thought. It knows nothing of your love, your history. The Andy you know is gone."

"*No*," Martin stamped his foot in the mud. "The boy's sick, but he ain't no monster. Even if he was, well...I've seen 'em in action. I've seen 'em come together, I've seen 'em bein' just as Human as the rest of us."

"Kessler, please. Do not let them deceive you, too."

"I'm done being deceived," Martin said, reaching for his revolver. The man leveled the barrel squarely at Talia's face.

Her eyes widened, then narrowed dangerously. "You would turn against your own kind? Against humanity?"

Martin scoffed. "I think humanity will be just fine without you."

CHAPTER 1
October 2015

Chop. Chop. Chop.

Martin Kessler spent his early morning chopping away at his mountains of firewood. The sound of his ax splitting logs cut through the quiet. Wiping the sweat off his brow, the old man took a moment to swig his thermos of ice cold water. He paused, his breath coming out in clouds, leaning on his ax and observing the pile he'd amassed. *Should be enough before breakfast,* he reckoned.

Martin stretched his arms over his head, feeling the satisfying pop of his joints. Afterwards, he stretched his calves, then his hamstrings, and then—

Kra-akk!

It felt like he'd been stabbed in the back, and in a way, he was— betrayed by his own aging body. A punch-like prickle shot through his spine, causing him to stumble. He muttered to himself, rubbing the sore spot.

Autumn's air nipped at Martin's exposed arms as he gathered his things. Yellows and reds mixed together in a harmony of crunchy leaves beneath his boots.

The baby blue paint that once vibrantly coated the home had faded over the years. It settled into the earth enough to appear as though it was a natural fixture, like it had sprouted from the ground after plenty of sun and water. Tall weeds crept and curled along the sides of the building. It had gone too long without proper care. The old man sighed, adding it to his mental list of chores.

It had been difficult to maintain the old property on his own. Martin's career with the local park rangers took up most of his time, and what little time he got to himself was dedicated to nothing but yard work, cooking and sleep. He already had to sell most of the critters they'd been taking care of, bringing a close to the family's long-running petting zoo; without his boy, Andy, there was no realistic way to keep it running smoothly.

Martin set his ax against the side of the home, the metal head sinking into the pebbles that lined its perimeter. Stepping in through the creaky front door, he set his leather hat on a rack immediately to his left, and ran a hand over his bald head. Sleepily, he shuffled toward the kitchen.

Fwoosh.

Propane crackled to light, blue flames blazing against the undersides of the burners. Martin cracked a couple of eggs into a butter-seasoned skillet. It wasn't anything impressive, but the aroma promised his growling stomach breakfast.

The eggs sizzled. Martin's thoughts drifted to the day ahead. He had a shift starting at noon, but before that, he'd hoped to make a grocery run. A scrawled list stuck to the fridge gave a few scant reminders: canned food, bulbs, paper towels, and, most importantly, feed for the remaining critters.

Dong. Dong.

Chimes rang from the living room grandfather clock. Martin flipped his eggs onto a china plate and set it down on the kitchen isle. He paused, looking outside. Morning mist still clung to the grass outside. The big maple tree out front gently swayed in the wind. Martin shuddered. He didn't want to think about driving through the fog.

A quiet creak rattled the settling house. Martin's attention drifted toward the upstairs, then to the papers on the counter. There was a pink truancy notice from the school, sat front and center. After all the trouble he went through to get her enrolled, Martin figured he should wake the girl. The bus would be pulling in soon.

He travelled through the hall, past dozens of forgotten photos. One always stood out among the others—a woman, with him and his son. Every time that woman passed his eye, he wondered for a moment.

Surely he'd remember her, such an important figure in his life. But every time her face crossed his mind, all he could draw was a fog.

And then, like that, the moment would pass. More pressing concerns were often at hand.

Aged wood groaned beneath his feet as he made his way upstairs. He approached Elena's bedroom door, its fresh coat of pink paint sticking out from the rest of the dreary hallway.

Martin knocked gently.

Silence greeted him.

The old man huffed and knocked again, a little more firm.

Still no answer.

The old man's hand hovered over the doorknob. He was going to have to go in to wake her, but he dreaded what would follow.

Twist. Creaaak.

He pushed the door open, sticking his head inside.

"Hey, girl. It's time for school."

The lump beneath the floral comforter stirred slightly, giving no further response. Martin stepped inside, the floorboards singing their mournful song.

"C'mon, now. You're gonna miss the—"

Whump.

A pillow struck his face before he could finish.

"Get out of my room," Elena said, hiding back beneath her sheets. Martin grunted, running a hand over his head. He'd expected resistance and all, but the pillow throwing? That was new.

They had been through this routine too many times to count at this point. It was all so tiring.

"Elena, please, not today," Martin said, picking the dormant pillow off the ground. By the time he rose again, Elena was back underneath the comforter. One could almost feel the anger permeating from beneath the floral print.

"We've been over this." Martin said.

"I don't care. I'm not going."

Martin massaged his eyeballs. "Elena."

"No!" the girl turned over, tightening the blanket around herself, a cornered snake coiling in its last effort of defense.

Martin's jaw tightened. His fingers twitched at his sides, his resolve crumbling just like the leaves outside. The ticking noise out in the hallway grew louder and louder. Each passing second was nothing but compounding stress.

The garish pink walls, the girl's hateful scribblings, the unicorn stickers, the shallow toy chest in the corner...

A Mr. Potato Head sat incomplete on a wooden chair. Its smile mocked the old man. He just about kicked the thing across the room.

With a deep breath, Martin gripped the edge of the comforter, yanking it back with enough force for Elena to roll out from under it. She screamed.

"I said *no!*"

Martin tossed the comforter aside. There was just the slightest wince on his end.

Elena lay curled in a tight ball, her pajamas rumpled and her long brown hair floating about due to the static electricity that was just created. She glared at the old man, her fingernails digging into her palms. A loud protest ensued. Elena was moved to tears.

Martin's face creased. He glanced out the window, the mist still clinging to everything like a ghost's bedsheets. Past the clearing,

Martin could just barely make out a flash of yellow approaching his home.

The bus was here already?

Grunting, the old man pulled open Elena's dresser drawers. He rifled through her neatly folded clothes, pulling out a pair of jeans with mismatched socks and a sweater. Martin placed them on the edge of the bed, then turned toward the door. Just outside, the bus was pulling into their gravel driveway.

"Get dressed." Martin said.

Heavy footsteps thumped down the stairs. Martin marched past his lukewarm eggs. Clearing his throat, he approached the yellow behemoth.

The bus wheezed to a halt, its door opening with a hydraulic hiss. Its driver leaned out, bulky frame barely contained on the tiny front seat. His face was obscured, a shadow cast by his Mountaineers hat in the early morning light. All Martin could make out were stained teeth surrounded by acne-covered lips. The man's large ears stuck out like satellite dishes from the sides of his head.

This wasn't their usual bus driver.

"Good morning, Mr. Kessler," the driver called out. "Is everything alright?"

Martin raised a brow. "Everything's fine, mister…?"

"Brown. Angstrom Brown."

Martin set his hands on his hips, looking around.

"Alright, *Mr. Brown.* Where's Mrs. Hendricks?"

"Mrs. Hendricks is on another route this morning. We had one of our guys call in sick. I'm filling in."

"Oh, is that right? You new in town?"

Brown's lips curled. "New? Oh no, Mr. Kessler. I've been 'round these parts for quite some time. Longer than you might think."

"Funny. Don't reckon I've seen you 'round before."

"Well, I reckon it's my first time doing this route." Brown let the word trail off for a few seconds. He laughed.

"So where is the little rascal?"

"She's—"

Donk.

Something thumped against the roof of the vehicle— Encyclopedia Animalis. It fluttered to a clumsy halt, flopping face-down in the dirt.

Andy's favorite, Martin thought. Just another tarnished memory to add to the list.

"I told you I'm not going!" Elena shouted from the upstairs window. She held a small pot of lilies above her head.

"Elena, don't you throw that!" Martin said.

"You're not Daddy," Elena bit back, tossing the pot at the bus. It shattered on impact, spreading dirt and plant matter all over the vehicle's pristine yellow coat. Brown laughed.

"*Feisty*, is she?" he asked.

"We'll be right out," Martin said. The old man stampeded back inside, his heavy boots thundering on the worn out steps. His jaw was clenched tight enough to crack a nut.

He burst into Elena's room, about ready to drag her out if necessary, but actually seeing the girl made him pause.

She sat cross-legged on her bed, shielding herself with her giant stuffed unicorn. The morning light filtering through the curtains cast a soft glow around the edges of her brown hair. It almost looked like a halo.

"Elena," Martin started, slowly. "You need to go say you're sorry to the bus driver."

"I don't want to," Elena said, voice muffled by the unicorn's fluff. "I want to go *home.*"

"Elena, this is not up for debate." Martin took a step forward. The girl's head snapped up. She raised the plushie in a threatening manner.

"Not another step! I'll throw this one too!"

The old man stopped. He could feel his blood pressure rising. His hand went over his eyes, then his nose. He slowly twisted the fleshy protrusion, trying to knead out the frustration.

Clearly he wasn't moving her anywhere. This was a problem. She needed to go to school. At this point, though, Martin couldn't bring himself to push her any more.

It was easier to be firm with the boy, he thought. *This was another beast entirely.*

Martin turned out the door, shaking his head intently.

"We're gonna have a little talk later, miss." he said. Elena blew raspberries in response. Martin bit his tongue and shut the door.

He supposed he should tell the bus driver the girl wasn't coming. Now he had to consider the next steps, what he could possibly do with this child, what he could say to the school...

As Martin reached the bottom of the stairs and turned the corner, his heart nearly stopped.

The hulking bus driver, Mr. Brown, was casually sifting through the family's belongings. His meaty fingers flipped through a yellowed photo album. A crooked grin spread on his face.

"Quite the collection you've got here, Mr. Kessler." Brown drawled, holding up a faded photograph. It depicted a stocky, ginger-headed boy with a pale complexion and a button nose— Andy. Brown gazed at the photo, his face exaggerated, comically confused.

"Who's this? Your boy? That's funny. He doesn't look like you."

Martin's fists clenched at his sides, turning white with the effort it took to restrain himself.

"Get out of my house." Martin growled.

Brown's grin widened. He lazily flipped through a few more pages of the album, eyes never quite leaving Martin's face.

"Now, now, is that any way to treat a guest?" Brown's rasp dripped with mock hurt. "I'm just trying to get to know you better. We're all friends here, aren't we?"

"I said, *get out.*" Martin repeated. The stranger chuckled in a way reminiscent of a cat choking. He let the scrapbook fall to the floor, cracking his neck.

Another step closer. Martin's eyes narrowed. He was about to start swinging when a movement outside the window caught his attention.

Somehow he hadn't caught it. The illusion had finally fallen. Brown had let in a bad draft or Martin's blood had run cold—either way, he felt frozen, as he watched a number of armored men, previously concealed, hopping out the back of the bus. The men quickly surrounded the property with practiced movements. Some of the men carried swords, axes and spears that glowed in the natural light—others came equipped with jet black crossbows which they aimed at the windows.

Brown laughed harder, drawing the old man's attention.

"Recognize your old friends, Kessler?" Brown asked. "The Order hasn't forgotten you."

Martin hadn't seen The Natural Order in some time. Of course, he'd always expected their eventual return, but *now?* What could they want, now?

His eyes darted around, cataloging potential weapons and escape routes. The shotgun was locked away in a safe downstairs, so too were his sidearms. Kitchen knives may have bought him a few seconds, but against trained knights in armor, they'd be little more than toothpicks.

Elena.

What was he going to do with Elena?

Martin weighed his options. The Order's men had the house surrounded. Upstairs, Elena likely remained unaware of the present danger.

He'd made a promise to protect her, and he was going to keep it.

"What do you want?" Martin asked.

"I want that little trinket you pocketed last fall, the one you thought we wouldn't miss," Brown said. "You hand it over, all nice and gentleman-like, and we'll be on our merry way. That sound like a bargain?"

No. Not that. Martin had nearly forgotten about the accursed thing. Tucked away upstairs—he couldn't let them have it. It was far too dangerous in their hands.

Then again, if he wouldn't cooperate, what would they do with him? With Elena?

His immediate thought was to tell a lie.

"That old thing," Martin said. "I sold it to a local pawn. Got a pretty penny too—"

Brown backhanded him, sending Martin into the dusty piano. It bellowed an uneasy tune as his full weight collided with it.

Just then, the knights outside shattered the windows with their hilts.

Martin pushed himself up and threw a punch at his attacker. Brown retaliated, grabbing Martin's arm, pulling him inward and kneeing him in the ribs.

The old man found himself wrestled to the ground. Brown pulled a rusty knife from his back pocket, placing the blade against Martin's wrist.

"Do you know what they did to thieves back then?" Brown asked. Martin responded with a headbutt, the back of his skull crushing the stranger's nose. Brown squealed and rolled off, Martin scrambling away toward the ocean of broken glass. Before he could make it very far, a knight stepped on one of his crawling hands. Martin wailed.

"*Idiot*," Brown said as he wiped the blood from his nose. "You've got nowhere to go. Tell me what I want to know, and I'll leave you alone. It's as simple as that."

Martin merely groaned in response. Brown shook his head, giving a small 'tut-tut.'

"Well if *you* don't remember where it is, maybe that charming half-breed upstairs does."

Martin's eyes widened.

"No," he said, struggling against the boot. "She don't know nothin'!"

Brown's yellow grin returned. "Oh? Then maybe you'd like to refresh your memory?"

"Listen to me. You *need* to listen to me. That thing, it's not what you think. It's dangerous. It's *evil*."

"We'll take it off your hands then, Kessler, free of charge. You know we specialize in exorcism?"

Martin's eyes shot around the room for any means of escape, any weapon, anything to get him out of this. The fireplace was nearby, if he could just get out from under this boot…!

With a burst of energy, he wrenched his hand free from the knight's heel, ignoring the glass digging into his palm. Martin dove for the poker, fingers closing around the cool metal, and in one fluid motion, he swung for Brown's head.

Brown weaved back, gracefully, the poker whooshing just past his face. Seizing the opportunity, he sent his meaty fist into Martin's jaw. The old man was sent back, stars exploding into view. Before he realized, he was tackled right through the glass coffee table.

The stranger's boot slammed into Martin's ribs with force, once, twice, three times, four times, over and over, again and again. Each impact forced the air from Martin's lungs. He curled into himself, trying to protect his organs, as the kicks continued to rain down.

"You should've just given it up, old man," Brown wheezed between his kicks. "'Cause now? Now I'm gonna hurt you. You *and* that little mongrel!"

Another firm kick to his sternum prevented a roar from erupting. As much as adrenaline had been flowing, his old bones had already given out. Gasping for air, panting, wheezing, Martin's gaze drifted upward.

No.

Just above, hiding behind the banister, Elena had been watching on for God-knows how long.

Martin tried to call out to her, to tell her to run, but all that escaped from his lips were weak, strangled groans. He could see his greatest failures play out in front of him. And then—darkness.

At that moment, Elena's world had narrowed to a point. The crashing and shouting faded to white noise. She breathed in short, tight gasps, unable to move.

"Spread out. I want this house searched top to bottom. Get me that girl too, if you find her," the stranger looked about before turning his gaze upward.

Their eyes locked. Time froze. Brown bared a predatory grin.

"'Ello, love."

Her survival instincts finally kicked in. She spun on her heel, bolting toward her room. The door slammed shut, Elena locking it behind herself. Heavy footsteps and angry shouts approached. The house shifted and bent with their weight.

Elena scanned her space. The window was her only escape route. She rushed over, small hands fumbling with the latch. The old wood creaked as she pulled it open. A gust of air greeted her. Elena leaned out and gauged the distance to the ground.

Was it too far to jump safely?

The little girl's gaze fell on the large maple tree just a few feet from the window, its branches stretching out like welcoming arms. Without a second thought, and because she heard banging at her door, Elena climbed onto the windowsill. She teetered precariously for but a moment before leaping toward the nearest branch.

Her hands grasped the tree bark, scraping her palms as she clung for dear life. The branch swayed, crackling ominously. Elena's heart leapt into her throat as she heard the splintering of wood—but not that of the branch—her bedroom door being kicked in. She swung her legs up and over, scrambling to pull herself to safety. From there, Elena inched along the limb until she reached the trunk From there, she made her way down.

Knights once more gathered on the lower floor, some emerging outside. Elena yelped and let herself drop the rest of the distance. Though the landing stung pretty hard, she was not about to be caught dead in her unicorn onesie. She sprinted to the garage, tackled the door open and slammed it shut, sure to lock it tight once more.

The musty scent of trash, old tools and sports equipment greeted her. Vision adjusted to the dark, she could barely make out Martin's old pickup truck sitting in the center. Without hesitation, she scrambled toward the driver's side door and pulled it open. She hoisted herself into the cab and settled in her seat.

On the other side of the garage door, Elena heard the knights pounding away, a few of them getting pretty close to knocking the thing off of its hinges. She immediately began a desperate search for the keys.

Where had she seen them, where had she seen them...?!

She checked the dashboard, the glovebox, the center console— *no, yeah, wait a minute*—Martin stashed them in the blinders, the old fool. Elena reached for the sun visor above her head and flipped it down.

A small cascade of items tumbled into her lap—a few old receipts, a crumpled map, and there, glinting beautifully in the low light, Martin's fabled keychain. Elena's fingers trembled, fumbling to insert the keys into the ignition. The dashboard lit up with a soft orange glow, and the old truck sputtered to life, rumbling like a sleeping beast waking from hibernation.

With a quick press of a keyring button, the garage door began to groan and creak, slowly rising to reveal the misty outdoors.

Elena's heart raced as she saw armored figures materializing on the other side of the raising door. She revved the engine, gripping the steering wheel tight. The truck roared in response. She revved it again, louder this time, wondering why the thing wouldn't go. Ah, right—the stick—she had to move it just a little ways down and—

VROOOOOM!

The truck shot forward, Elena getting whiplash as she shot back. She slammed her foot on the gas and braced. The truck lunged ahead once more, tires squealing against the concrete before grinding up gravel.

Elena did her best to swing the steering wheel around as she approached the bus stationed just outside. Knights scattered out of the way like bowling pins, the truck's front bumper clipping the side of one unfortunate soldier. He was sent tumbling across the driveway in a clumsy clatter. Elena winced, though her foot remained firmly on the gas pedal.

She pulled the wheel to the right. The truck's tires dug into the soft earth of the front lawn, kicking up clods of grass and mud that spattered its underside. The world tilted sickeningly as the truck leaned precariously on two wheels, threatening to topple over at any moment. Elena shifted her weight to the left and throttled the gas pedal. The truck landed back on all fours, the driver's side mirror clipping on the bus's back corner.

The truck barreled down the dirt road, kicking up clouds of dust in its wake. Mist clung to its windshield, obscuring the girl's view further, but she didn't dare slow down.

Through the haze, Elena could make out the faint outlines of towering cornstalks ahead of her. The sea of green and gold stretched as far as the eye could see. Tranquil, pleasant, a major contrast to the chaos she just bore witness to. Suddenly, another flash of yellow caught her eye—a second school bus was approaching the intersection ahead. Elena's eyes widened as she realized she was on a collision course for the vehicle.

In a split second decision, she jerked the wheel to the left, the side of the red pickup scraping against the bus's front bumper, and giving poor Mrs. Hendricks a scare. The truck went careening off the road, into the ditch, and plowed through the cornfield ahead.

Going, going…
Gone.

CHAPTER 2

A softball whistled through the air before making a cushy landing in one's leather mitt. Taking the ball out, Andy Kessler took a few steps back before throwing it back with all his might. It zipped across the lush field into the hands of Vick Roldán, who caught it with ease.

The two boys must have been a football field's length apart, yet they tossed the ball back and forth to one another like it was a casual game of catch. To them, perhaps, it was.

Andy was a Werewolf, with a shaggy ginger mullet just a few decades out of date. His pointed ears twitched, eyes focused on his companion across the field.

"What're you writin' about this week?" Andy asked. Vick rolled the ball between his slender fingers.

"I'm running a bit short on story ideas, I'll be honest. I'm thinking of maybe covering something for the fall festival, *maybe*, but besides that…I dunno." the Vampire tossed the softball up in the air, catching it, and throwing it right back. Though scrawny in build, he was quite strong—perhaps even stronger than Andy—although such was typical for his kind.

"Well, I'm sure you'll think of somethin'," Andy said, catching the ball with an oomph. "You know, actually, Mr. Fizetti said somethin' about a new location last time we ate there."

"Really? The old diner?" Vick asked.

Andy nodded, tossing the ball back. "Yeah. Mr. Hudson had mentioned somethin' to him about health code violations in the building, and like…well you know, it's an apartment, so he can't really control what the tenants do?"

"My money's on it being Drew's place."

"Yeah," Andy said, sticking his tongue out with playful disgust. "I think that could be a cool story, though. Mr. Fizetti's, I mean."

Vick nodded. He approached from across the field.

"I could probably hit him up before the festival if I'm lucky." Vick said.

"You bringin' anyone to the dance?"

Vick chewed on the thought. He brought a hand to his ice-pick nose. *Sniffle.*

"Somethin' wrong?" Andy asked.

"Nothing, just, uh…*huh*. Guess I hadn't thought about that yet," Vick shrugged his shoulders. Almost without thinking, he continued. "Hey, maybe the two of us could go."

He hadn't meant for it to be anything more than a casual suggestion between friends, but the implications lingered, like stink clouds muddying up their casual atmosphere.

Andy raised an eyebrow and cracked a slight smile. "What?"

"You know," Vick brought his claws to the back of his neck. "Just like, go together. As friends. I mean, the girls do it all the time."

"Uh, yeah. Why not? Could be fun."

"Sweet. Should we wear matching outfits?"

"Might be a bit much."

"Maybe for you."

Definitely, Andy thought. The boy only had one 'suit' to begin with, an oversized blazer with matching checkerboard pants. Non-garish attire wasn't exactly cheap.

The faint jingling of a bicycle bell rang out across the field. Andy turned to see a purple exoskeleton speeding toward them, kicking up a trail of dust and leaves.

Cici the Xita perched on the seat, bringing the bike to a skidding stop. Her four arms gripped the handlebars, her single enormous eye unblinking.

"Hey guys," Cici chirped. "What's up?"

"Just playin' ball." Andy said. "Talkin' about the dance."

"Ooh, you find who you're going with?"

"Somethin' like that."

As the dust settled, the boys noticed another figure seated on the back of the bike. Tanya O'Mally, an Elf and distinguished member of the Rangers, clung to Cici's midsection. Her plum coiled hair bounced above her shoulders as she turned her head. Fierce as always, her eyes locked with Andy's.

Vick turned his head to Cici. "Isn't she like…supposed to be on duty?"

Tanya climbed off the bike, shooting Vick a dangerous look. Her arms crossed, and she blew a loc of hair from her face.

"She snuck out." Cici said. "I may have encouraged her a little. It's too nice of a day to be cooped up in a watchtower."

Andy shook his head. "You're gonna get her in trouble one of these days."

Another dirty look. Andy gulped in response, point taken.

"So, you guys up for a little adventure?" Cici asked.

"Depends what kind of adventure we're talkin' about." Andy said.

"Well, Tanya thought it would be cool for us all to go to her place and hang out for a bit. Just us, no adults, no rules, no holds barred." Cici threw a few punches at the end.

"Is that a good idea?" Andy asked, turning to Tanya. "Ranger territory is off limits for citizens."

"Yeah, if you're a *lame* Ranger. Tanya's cool." Cici grabbed Tanya by both shoulders as she said this. The Elf squirmed a bit.

"Nobody's gonna come looking for us?" Andy asked.

"No, man. Not unless there's like, an emergency or something."

Andy looked to Vick, gauging his reaction—more than okay with it, going by his lazy smile.

"Alright, sure. Long as we ain't steppin' on any toes." Andy said.

"Great! Let's bounce!" Cici said.

The group set off, Cici leading the way on her bike. Andy and Tanya trailed behind in long strides in an attempt to keep pace. Vick floated, as usual.

The afternoon sun filtered through the dying leaves. Orange shadows covered the paths ahead.

Scenery gradually shifted from the cobblestone roads to dirt paths. These paths would give way to no path at all, nothing beyond beaten grass. Dense clusters of trees quickly replaced many neat rows of quaint homes and businesses.

Vick, focused on flying, gradually caught up with Cici. He turned himself over into a basking position, arms behind his head, legs crossed. He positioned himself adjacent to the bike.

"So, are you excited for the festival tomorrow?" Vick asked.

Cici's antennae perked at the question. "Oh, yeah! I've been working on my costume for weeks. It's gonna blow your freakin' mind."

"Is it a butterfly again?"

Cici rolled her eye.

"No, it's not a butterfly again."

"Does she do butterflies often?" Andy spoke up from the back.

"Every other year." Vick said.

"I've done it like, twice." Cici said. "And it's not like you haven't reused a costume before. How many times have you worn that cheap Dracula outfit?"

Andy laughed out loud. "Dracula? Ain't that…offensive?"

"Not if a Vampire does it, no," Vick said, as if it was obvious.

"Still. Is that like a problem you guys…that *we* have? People dressing up like monsters and stuff?"

Cici shook her head. "Not really. These days, costumes are all about pop culture and repping whatever's the most fresh."

"Do you remember the year Brethren Clown came out?" Vick asked. Cici laughed.

"Yeah! Yeah, like that."

Andy tilted his head. "Brethren Clown?"

"Have you not seen it?" Cici's jaw went agape, and she clasped her hands together. "Okay. Okay, we have to show him."

"It's a masterpiece." Vick said.

"Dude, it sucks so much," Cici said with a snort.

"So much."

"I still don't know what it is." Andy said.

"We'll get you up to speed, don't worry." Vick replied.

The group continued into the woods; the trees growing denser, their spreading branches like fingers trying to grab at their heads. After about an hour of walking, they came upon a large tunnel, filled with thorns. Andy remembered well enough as one of the few entrances to the valley—a small mob of The Natural Order previously burned its innards away. He was relieved to see it was restored…if not feeling rather existential about it.

He really *was* trapped in this valley, wasn't he?

Tanya placed her hand on the thorns, energy flowing through her fingertips and into the bramble. Roots gave a shriek of protest and retracted, opening up the cave for the group to enter. The tunnel went all the way through the mountain. Light pooled in, the roots further retreating into their craters. The group carefully stepped forward.

Emerging on the other side, the group shielded their eyes, coming out underneath a breezy canopy which Andy had some passing familiarity with—this was around where he got caught snooping around the city's borders just over a year ago.

Nervously, Andy checked over his shoulder to make sure Tanya wasn't planning an ambush. As she usually did when making eye contact with Andy, the Elf cracked a dominant smile. The boy shook.

In the center of the upcoming clearing was a tall tree with a naturally generated home sticking out of it. The trunk was wrapped in a thick vine which acted like a ladder, pink blossoms sprouting from various points along the way.

It was just as Andy remembered it—his first interrogation, right here. He found it strange, in retrospect, how he'd now been invited to the home under much friendlier circumstances.

Tanya approached the towering tree, gripping the vines and climbing her way up, followed by the others. Cici climbed up with ease, four arms working in coordination. Vick merely floated to the top, making the entire ordeal seem effortless. Andy was the slowest, as per usual.

As they got 'upstairs,' Tanya pushed aside the leather curtains and directed the others toward the living room.

The inside was cozy, spacious. Soft light shone through the leafy curtains, painting the room a muted green. The windows were all a slightly different shape from one another, none of them quite perfect squares. Three large bean bag chairs surrounded a stump in the center of the room. Scattered around were a few training weights and bristly brushes.

The one new addition Andy could spot was an old CRT television in the corner, with an attached video game console. He was going to give himself two guesses of who made *that* contribution. It might have been a wonder how they got electricity out here to begin with, before Andy realized the thing wasn't even plugged in anywhere.

Cici must've gone through all that trouble to lug it out here only to realize it would be virtually useless. *Poor thing.* Andy thought it cruel to giggle at the thought, continuing his walk around the home with a suppressed smile.

Vick was already sinking into one of the beanbag chairs. Tanya sat at the edge of the central stump. Andy hadn't even had a moment to secure a spot before Cici sprung into action. She always had to keep the group entertained, it seemed.

"Hey gang, let's do a game! Like uh…charades!"

Andy slightly scowled, whereas Vick outwardly groaned. Tanya was the only one that looked remotely open to the idea, but that was enough validation for Cici to go off on. She continued, squatting and putting her arms out in front of herself. One of her hands imitated the throttle of a motorbike.

Just then, the group could hear the revving of an engine outside. Cici, in a state of shock, examined her hands—Vick quickly crushed her dreams of wizardry.

"Guys, *look*," Vick said, getting to his feet and running to the window. The others followed suit. Crowding around, their eyes all widened at the coming sight. A battered pickup truck came barreling into the clearing, engine roaring like a wounded beast. The vehicle swerved wildly, flat tires tossing up clumps of dirt and grassy roots. It was careening right toward Tanya's home.

At the last possible moment, the truck's brakes screeched. It came to a muddy halt, gently bumping into the base of the tree. A shower of leaves fell from the branches above, like celebratory confetti for the momentous occasion.

Andy could recognize that truck anywhere—his dad's. However, it wasn't his old man that hesaw behind the wheel of the vehicle. No, he...he really *couldn't* see anyone driving at all.

Tanya had already moved out the door, climbing down the trunk to investigate. The driver's side door swung open. The Elf took a defensive stance, pulling a knife from her belt. As soon as the driver hopped out onto the ground, however, the knife dropped.

Sniffling, trembling, Elena ran right into Tanya's arms, hugging her tight. Tanya ran her hand through the little girl's head of hair. She looked over at Andy somewhat expectantly. Blinking, the boy approached and crouched beside them. If only he wasn't so beside himself to begin with.

Where did he even start? Of course, he should comfort the girl, but...*if she was here, in Martin's old pickup, that could only mean...*

No. That was too extreme of a conclusion to jump to so soon. Andy shook the notion out of his head. His eyes locked with Elena's.

"Uh…hey, bud," Andy muttered. "You okay? What's goin' on?"

The little girl sobbed, burying her face into Tanya's tunic. Andy shifted in his stance before trying again. He figured if he could make himself appear smaller, maybe she wouldn't be so intimidated.

"Elena, right? You remember me?"

The little girl nodded her head, though her expression suggested her memory of the boy was quite bitter. Andy let out a soft sigh.

"Can you tell us what happened?"

Elena hiccuped and wiped her nose on Tanya's tunic—the Elf did everything in her power to ignore this.

"It was scary." Elena said. Andy nodded.

"Yeah? What was scary, Elena?"

"Bad men came to the house."

"Bad men?" Andy squinted.

"They hurt Mr. Kessler. They had swords, there were so many of them. They broke the windows and came inside. The big man kept asking Mr. Kessler for something. He said Mr. Kessler took it last fall. He wouldn't tell them where it was, so…so they kept hitting him."

Andy's nostrils flared, the hair on the back of his neck standing on end.

"Did you see what happened to Mr. Kessler after that?" Andy asked, his voice strained. Elena shook her head.

"No. I ran away after that."

"Okay." Andy said. "Thank you, Elena."

Tanya placed a hand on Andy's shoulder. She gave him a nod of encouragement before turning her attention back to Elena, placing a hand on the little girl's head.

Cici and Vick made their way down the side of the treehouse, hovering nearby. Their eyes went wide when they took it in—a Human trembling in Tanya's arms.

Cici's eye blinked rapidly. Vick's face was paler than normal.

"How'd she get here?" he asked.

"The truck, I reckon." Andy pointed with his thumb.

Cici took a step forward, shaking with excitement. "This is incredible! Look how small she is! How squishy she looks! I didn't know you guys came this smooth."

Andy shot Cici a warning look. "Cool it. She's been through somethin' rough. We ought to give her some space."

Cici's antennae drooped. "Oh, right. Sorry."

Andy did his best to process all the information he'd just heard, pacing back and forth while Tanya comforted the child.

Martin, attacked by armed men, asking for something he'd taken last fall...more pressingly, was his dad even still alive?

A growl uncomfortably fizzled in Andy's throat, his body tensing. For the child's sake, he forced himself to stay calm.

"We need to get help." Andy eventually said. "For her and... *and* my dad."

Vick nodded, his eyes still trained to the little girl. "Yeah, about that...we can't just walk her into town like this."

Andy let out an annoyed grunt, thinking to himself, before he turned to Tanya.

"You got any blankets?"

CHAPTER 3

Various passersby exchanged confused looks and glances. The group tried to pay them no mind.

At the center of their precession was a small figure completely shrouded in a fuzzy blue blanket. Someone cut two round holes for the entity's green eyes to peek out of.

Andy walked close to Elena's obscured form, occasionally giving her a guiding hand when she stumbled or wandered off too far. The blanket dragged on the cobblestone, already fraying and picking up dirt. Tanya continued her look of repose as she tried to ignore the gradual destruction of her property.

As they passed the town square, a group of children playing marbles stopped to stare.

"Look! A ghost!" one said with glee. His companions crowded around Elena for a better view. The little girl froze, trembling beneath the sheet.

Andy very quickly dispersed the meddling group with a wave of his claws.

"Alright, alright, move it. Ain't you never seen a ghost before?" Andy said. The kids scattered, giggling. Andy rolled his eyes and kept going, hurrying Elena along with a hand on her back.

Just coming up in the distance, the group beheld Hudsonville's city hall, a grand, blocky structure with a large stained-glass eye as its centerpiece. The building's harsh grey angles and stark shapes stood out among the colorful buildings of the city. It was high and above the town, a panopticon keeping the Supernatural settlement in line.

'Freaky looking,' as the local youth would describe it. Andy knew full well what lay beyond those large heavy doors at this point, but he couldn't help but think one of these days the building was going to eat him alive.

Taking a deep breath in, he pushed open the doors.

The interior was pleasant, despite the dismal outside. Soft light buzzed from an overhead chandelier, casting fractal shadows onto the marble floor. Spacious, airy, the lobby was minimally decorated with a few odd plants and paintings. Large blocky columns stood supporting the ceiling above.

To the right, Andy spotted a set of double doors leading to the Moonlit Ward, a spot he would visit at least once a month. Inside was a safe place for Werewolves like him to spend their nights adjusting to their condition. Cici informed Andy that they've made pretty good progress with his alter ego as of late; apparently, 'Rex,' as he called himself, really enjoyed professional wrestling on TV. *Go figure.*

To the left were the double doors to the archives, a library which covered just about everything to do with local history. If someone inked a document in Hudsonville, it could be found there.

Close to those doors was the entrance to a spiral staircase, and close to that, a gold-latticed elevator that looked a bit too old-fashioned to properly function.

Near the back of the room, a zen waterfall trickled soothingly behind the reception desk, where a studious shadow clacked away at her keyboard.

The receptionist, an Onierovore, Snoozie, raised her sail-shaped head. Six glowing green eyes appeared to greet the approaching children.

"Heya, kiddos! What brings you in today?"

Andy cleared his throat. "Uh, hey, Snoozie. We've got a bit of a situation here."

Snoozie's eyes drifted to the small blanketed figure, then back at Andy. There was no use trying to hide anything from the woman—she could read their minds like picture books. Sighing, Andy pulled back the makeshift disguise, revealing Elena's puzzled expression. Snoozie blinked.

"Oh my, is that...?"

Andy nodded. "Elena Davis. She just showed up on the outskirts of town, looking for help." Pausing, his fists clenched in and out. "Some men came and hurt my dad."

"Oh, Andy," Snoozie said while shaking her head. "I'm so sorry."

"It's fine, just...is Mr. Davis still here? I think they'll probably want to see each other. Maybe we can figure out what to do next."

"Mr. Davis is in holding downstairs. I'm not supposed to let anybody in without clearance, but..."

The Onierovore took in Elena's puppy dog expression and huffed.

"...I think we can make an exception, just this once. Follow me, and stay close."

Snoozie's body uncoiled from behind the desk and she slithered out to join the group. They followed her into the elevator. Slowly the mechanism was lowered into the bowels of City Hall.

Andy's leg bounced up and down, hands gripping the railings. He could feel his stomach drop along with the carriage.

Butch Davis was the one who killed Andy's mother, as well as the Werewolf who infected him. It was a misguided act of revenge, after Martin had mistaken Butch's son—Elena's father—for a wild grizzly bear. The particular series of events had thrown his entire life out of whack. Seeing him again, even a year after everything happened...Andy wasn't sure if he was ready for it.

"You okay?" Cici asked. Andy gave a weak thumbs up. After he recovered, the group followed Snoozie down a dusty corridor, lined with cells.

Cici couldn't help but peek at each one as they passed. Most were empty. In one, a corpse-like Grim sat on her bedside, softly sighing. She hardly lifted her head when the group made their pass.

Another cell had what appeared to be a writhing mass of worms in the form of a person. They squirmed and squelched as their wormy legs paced back and forth. Vick ogled at this one too—he wondered why they didn't just break apart and crawl out between the bars. Did this insectoid hivemind understand and, more importantly, respect the impromptu judicial system instilled by Hudson? Vick added it to his potential to-do list of interviews.

Elena stood at Tanya's side, the two of them lingering at the back of the group. Her onesie continued to accumulate grime from the floor. It smelled funny down here. Funny and sad. The girl's nose wrinkled, and she clung to Tanya tighter.

Just before the end of the hall, Snoozie came to a halt. She cleared her throat as she turned to face the cell on the left.

"Excuse me, Mr. Davis? You have a visitor."

A lone figure sat hunched in the center, his back turned. His broad shoulders slumped. The once-imposing man looked rather defeated, a shadow of his former glory as an Elder of the Rangers. Tanya's lip curled with some contempt, but as usual, she remained quiet.

Butch hardly responded to Snoozie's initial greeting, but his head turned as he picked up on a familiar scent.

Sniff.

Sniff, sniff.

Muscles tense, he faced the group, eyes landing on Elena. Disbelief, fury, confusion, they all quickly cycled through the man's tired face. He crawled toward the bars, remaining at eye level with the girl.

"Elena? What are you…? *Why* are you here?" Butch looked up at Andy for an explanation. The boy gulped.

32

"The farm was attacked. Natural Order, from the sounds of it. They was after somethin' my dad took."

"What did he take?"

Andy crossed his arms. "That's what we're tryin' to figure out."

Somewhat unsatisfied with the answer, Butch turned his focus back to his granddaughter. His large hand poked through the bars and carefully caressed her hair.

"Did you come here all on your own?"

Elena nodded. Butch sighed.

"You know you were supposed to stay away."

"I can't. Not from you, Grandpa."

Andy shifted his weight from foot to foot, his brow furrowed in thought. It was so stuffy. This place made him feel trapped. He cleared his throat.

"Mr. Davis, sir, we ought to figure out what to do with Elena now that she's here. It ain't safe for her to go back home."

Butch stroked his stubble, deep in thought. "You're right, but… where *can* she go? This town ain't for Humans, 'specially not little ones."

Cici's eye gleamed. "Oh! She could stay with me! I've got a spare room in the hive, I promise I won't let any of my cousins eat her!" She paused for a moment. "That sounded bad."

Butch grimaced. "Yeah."

"She could always stay with my old man and I." Vick offered.

"With as much as she talks, I especially don't want her around you, Roldán." Butch said.

Vick shrugged. "Yeah, alright."

"Could she stay with the Rangers?" Snoozie asked. Butch shook his head.

"I would rather she didn't be around that environment."

Andy shifted his weight again. He couldn't believe he was about to suggest this, but…

"What if…what if she stayed with *me?*"

The group turned to look at him. Andy continued before he lost his nerve.

"I mean, I've got room. Mr. Hudson lent me his old cabin, and…I know how to take care of her. I helped raise plenty of critters back home, yeah? Plus, I'm probably the most adjusted to Human society out of any of us. I could keep her safe."

Butch's bald brow furrowed. The hall went quiet enough for the group to hear the distant drip of a leaky faucet. Elena looked between her grandfather and Andy, her small hand still clutching Tanya's. After what felt like an eternity, Butch spoke.

"You know…that might not be such a bad idea."

Andy blinked. "Really?"

"You've saved her life before."

Had he? All he did was not *shoot* the man when he had the chance. Was sparing her that trauma really deserving of praise?

"*Whatever* you think, you've earned my trust." Butch said, as if reading the boy's mind. He turned his attention to Elena, face softening.

"What do you think about that? Would you be okay staying with Andy for a while?"

Elena sniffled. "I don't know. I want to stay with you."

Butch's attempted to mask with a smile.

"I know you do, sweetheart. But it's not very nice here. I know this isn't what you wanted, but sometimes life ain't about what you want, it's working with what you have. Remember that time we found the little baby bird that fell from its nest?"

Elena sniffled. "You said we couldn't keep it."

"That's right. Do you remember why?"

"Because it had to learn to fly on its own?"

"Exactly." Butch smiled, ruffling Elena's hair a little. "You need to learn how to live life on your own. Sometimes you need to take big risks. You gotta jump if you're gonna learn how to fly. Andy here, he's a good kid. He'll take good care of you for now. And who knows? Maybe you two will have fun together."

Elena looked at Andy, wiping her nose. The boy cleared his throat and did his best to match Butch's energy.

"Uh…yeah. My cabin's right on the lake. We can go fishin' if you want, or have picnics on the shore. There's a community garden pretty close by too where we can pick our own fruits and veggies. I've also got a kitty-cat." Andy paused. "You ain't scared of kitty-cats, are you?"

Elena shook her head. "No."

"Alrighty then," Andy gave another awkward thumbs up, and eyed Butch for confirmation. The girl, though slightly puzzled, responded to her grandfather with muted enthusiasm.

"Okay. I'll stay with Andy."

Butch smiled. "Atta girl. Then I'll see you real soon, alright?"

"Okay."

Elena hugged Butch through the bars one last time before stepping back. Andy gave her a brief pat on the back, hands shooting back into his pockets. His lips pressed thin as he made eye contact with the old Ranger.

"Don't worry, Mr. Davis. I promise I'll take good care of her."

"I know you will."

As the group turned to leave, Butch called out one last time. "Andy, wait."

"Sir?"

"Whatever Martin took from The Order, it must be important for them to have tracked him down. Be careful. Whatever it is they're planning…"

Andy gave a firm nod. "Yes, sir."

With that, Andy and company made their way back to the elevator, Elena's small hand clasped still in Tanya's. The boy's mind raced. *What had his father gotten himself mixed up in? And more importantly, was Martin even still alive?*

The responsibility he had, as well as the many facets of uncertainty which surrounded it, was heavy. Not only was he going to have to figure out what happened to Martin, but he was also in charge of caring for a Human girl…

In a magic city…

Full of monsters.

They weren't *all* that bad, of course. Andy knew that well enough after living here for a while. Still though, it might be a lot—he wasn't so much as concerned for Elena's reaction to the citizens as he was the citizens' reaction to her.

Snoozie turned to address the group as they made their way into the lobby.

"Alright, kids. I think it would be best if Andy and Elena went straight home tonight. Andy, try to keep her out of sight as much as possible until we figure out a more permanent solution."

Andy nodded. "Thanks, Snoozie. We'll be careful."

Pulling Tanya's blanket back over Elena's head, Andy led the group out the front doors and back into the city streets.

"Guess we should call it a day." Vick said. "You good from here, Andy?"

Andy nodded. "Yeah, I think so. We'll head straight to my place and get her settled in."

Cici bounced up and down. "Can I come visit? I wanna show Elena my bugs."

"Maybe another day. You guys have that fall festival thing tomorrow, don't you?"

Vick tilted his head. " '*You guys?*' Andy, are you not going?"

"I don't know," Andy said. "I'm not sure if I'm really feeling up for it anymore."

"Fall festival?" Elena asked from under her shroud. Andy winced.

"It's basically the big Halloween celebration they have every year. There's games, food, costumes, dancing—all kinds of stuff."

Elena's eyes lit up. "That sounds cool! Can we go?"

"I don't know, Elena, I don't think it's safe for you to be around so many people right now."

"I can blend in, I promise I'll be good and stay hidden! Pretty please?"

Andy hesitated, glancing at his friends. They all simultaneously shrugged.

"It could be fun." Vick said. "We could all keep an eye on her."

"Yeah," Cici chimed in. "I bet we could come up with an *awesome* disguise."

Tanya looked on at Andy expectantly. He…never really could get a read on her. Assumedly, she was joining in on the peer pressure. A smirk graced her lips.

Andy rubbed the back of his neck. On one hand, taking Elena to a crowded festival seemed like exactly the kind of thing Snoozie just told him *not* to do. On the other hand…maybe it will help take Elena's mind off everything that happened. As long as they were careful…

"Alright," Andy relented. He crouched by Elena and put his hands on her shoulders. "But you gotta do what we say when we say so, okay? And no runnin' off on your own."

Elena nodded aggressively, her blanket just about flying off her head. Andy's stabilization is all that kept it in place.

"I will, I promise! Thank you, Andy!"

Andy stood back up, feeling proud of himself, despite his resignation. At least she was happier now.

"Guess we'll see you all tomorrow, then." Andy said. "Meet at my place around noon?"

The others nodded, Andy bumped fists with them, and the group parted ways for the evening.

As Andy and Elena walked through the darkening streets toward his cabin, he kept a firm hand on her shoulder, guiding her along.

"So…do you like Halloween?" Andy asked, trying to make conversation.

"I think it's kind of silly." Elena replied. Andy scoffed.

"Silly? Yeah. I guess. But you do get a bunch of free goodies, what, for dressin' up a little? I'd say that's a pretty good deal."

Elena giggled and skipped ahead, Andy doing his best to keep up.

"Speaking of dressing up," Andy continued. "What do you wanna be?"

Elena rubbed her chin, deep in thought. Her eyes slowly panned toward the slicked back hair of a passing stranger. A lightbulb went off inside her head. She proudly pointed a finger in the air.

"I wanna be a Vampire!"

CHAPTER 4

Drew Warren woke with a start, eyes blinking open to harsh light. He groaned, feeling the uncomfortable crunch of potato chips beneath him, his skin sticking to the hot leather couch.

Fragments of last night's binge session came back in flashes. Monster trucks, energy drinks, an ungodly amount of greasy food…

He sat himself upright, sending a cascade of cans tumbling to the floor. His arms stretched above, Drew cringing as his back popped and cracked. A power dampening cuff on his wrist reflected the morning sun into his one good eye. Drew growled. Just another example of the proverbial 'man' trying to keep him in check.

Drew stumbled to his feet, kicking aside empty soda cans and takeout containers. The small space was in complete disarray, clothes strewn about, posters peeling off the walls, dubious paraphernalia scattered across every surface.

Not watching his step, Drew stepped on a spiked wristband with his bare foot. He yelped, hopping around and gripping his sole. It wasn't long before he lost his balance and collided with the nightstand. Another cascade of miscellaneous items. Drew cursed to himself over and over, before going to pick it up.

The first mess of many, today. Drew slid open his closet door, rifling through a crumpled pile of crop-tops, denim jackets and baggy jeans. He pulled out a wrinkled graphic t-shirt, a faded skull front and center. After a brief smell check, he put it on.

As he got dressed, Drew caught a glimpse of himself in the cracked mirror hanging in his closet door. His long, red hair was sticking up every which way except where it needed to be. The scar over his left eye stood out stark from his sickly skin. He dragged his fingers through his bangs, using them to cover the blemish as best as he could before applying some hairspray.

Making his way to the tiny kitchen, Drew kicked aside some more trash. He opened the fridge, finding it mostly empty, save for a half-eaten burrito of questionable age. Drew grabbed a soda can, punched a hole in it with one of his claws, and drank the whole thing in one go. Finished, he crushed it and tossed the painted aluminum over his shoulder.

He contemplated whether he should actually attempt to clean or go back to sleep, when a sharp knock at the door stirred him awake.

Drew stumbled toward the door, yanking it open. He squinted against the bright light of the outside hall.

"What?" he asked.

Cici stood in the doorway, eye wide. She clutched a large bag of beef jerky in two of her hands, while her other two arms cradled a bulging backpack.

"Hey, Drew. Brought some snacks," Cici held up the jerky. "I thought we could hang out before the festival tonight!"

Before the man could accept, Cici pushed past, freezing up once she realized what she was looking at.

"Dang, bro. Do you *live* like this?"

Drew turned a bright red. "Uh, yeah. What about it?"

"When's the last time you cleaned up around here?"

"I dunno. Couple weeks, tops."

Cici sighed. "Look, I know things are a little...*rough,* but this *can't* be good for you."

Drew's shoulders tensed, but he didn't let the comment sting too bad. This *was* Cici after all—she was like a little sister to him, ever since he arrived as a teenager. Sure, it felt a bit weird sometimes, especially considering the gap in their ages. Suppose, though, it didn't really bug either of them at the end of the day.

"I'm fine." Drew muttered. "Just been busy, is all."

"Busy doing what? Feeling sorry for yourself?"

"Hey, I don't need a lecture, alright? I've just been getting ready for the concert."

Cici brushed a few chips off the couch before taking a seat. "You're really hung up on that, huh?"

"Of course I am," Drew paced back and forth. "This is what, like, the first time in five years they're letting me perform anywhere? If I bomb this…" the man pinched the bridge of his nose. "God, Cici. People already think I'm a loser, what if this just cements that?"

"Hey, c'mon now," Cici patted the crumb-covered seat to her side. "You're not a loser, and you're not gonna bomb. You've been practicing, right?"

Drew nodded, slumping down onto the couch. "Yeah. Whenever I can get everyone together."

"Well, there you go. Practice makes perfect. Your show is gonna be perfect!"

"What happens when it's not?"

Cici shrugged. "Then we'll cross that bridge. But, honestly, I don't think we will."

"Yeah…ugh. Ugh! I dunno."

"That's okay." Cici gave him a few pats on the shoulder before returning her hands to her lap. Clearly, just talking about the show was stressing the poor guy out.

"So are you dressing up tonight?"

Drew reached for a piece of jerky, gnawing on it. "Ehh, maybe. Probably just going to do some face paint. I'm thinkin' like…The Crow, or Sting, or something."

"Ohhh, Crow could be cool. You'd have to dye your hair again, though."

Drew pursed his lips. "True. What are you going as?"

"Oh! Well…I kinda want it to be a surprise."

"Surprise, huh? You been workin' on it long?"

"Uhuh! Hand sewn!"

"You sew now?"

"Uncle Bisby does, remember?"

Drew laughed. "Oh, yeah. Well, that's pretty cool. I'm sure whatever you came up with is gonna be awesome."

"Thanks! Yeah, I'm really excited to show everyone. So uh…" Cici looked around the room. What little expression her rigid face could pull off indicated some sort of scowl.

"Do you like…want help cleaning up?"

Drew's smile faded away. "Nah, it's fine. I'll get to it."

And though he made it clear he wasn't interested, Cici got started anyways. Drew watched on with an irritated expression as she gathered the scattered trash. He knew she wanted to help, but part of him resented the implication that he couldn't take care of himself.

"You really don't have to do this," Drew grumbled, shoving a pizza box into a large garbage bag.

"I know. But that's what friends are for, right?" Cici said.

As they worked, the apartment slowly looked less and less like a disaster zone, and more like a place of living. Now, it certainly could use a good go-over with a vacuum cleaner and a feather duster, but at least the bulk of the junk was now tucked away in the trash bags piled near the front door.

Cici talked away about her excitement, filling Drew in on the latest town gossip all the while. Despite his sultry mood, Drew found himself relaxed as the two of them continued their conversation. On the other hand, he could feel the pangs of a headache coming on real soon...

"Oh!" Cici exclaimed. "I almost forgot, you know, the weirdest thing happened yesterday."

"Yeah?" Drew asked, half listening. He was clawing a flaky stain on the coffee table.

"Yeah. Long story short, Andy's taking care of a *Human* now."

Drew's head snapped up. "A *what?*"

Cici nodded with tempered excitement. "I know, right? Apparently there was some kind of attack, and so she ran here looking for her granddad. Andy's taking care of her now."

Considering that kid's questionable decision-making skills, Drew didn't like it. The last time he gave Andy the benefit of the doubt, well, Andy nearly got his whole town killed.

"Is that really a good idea?"

"Elder Davis seemed to think so."

Drew shook his head. "I don't like it. Humans don't belong here, *especially* not kids."

"I mean, she can't exactly go back home right now. And, Andy's probably the most qualified to look after her, yeah?"

"Yeah, right. Andy doesn't know the first thing about raising kids."

"I dunno, he says he's 'reared a few goats,' or something."

"That's not the same thing."

Cici shrugged. "Well, what do you care? He seems responsible."

"I don't know. I don't trust it. What happens when they get the all clear? She just gonna be sent back out into the Human world? What happens if she starts running her mouth?"

"I don't think that really matters at this point. They already know we're here."

"Yeah…they do, don't they?" Drew huffed, leaning back on the couch. He pawed at the breast pocket of his jacket for a paper box, sticking a fresh cigarette in between his lips.

"Why do you think they've waited so long?"

"For what?"

"Before attacking again?" Drew sat up. He took a deep drag while contemplating the thought. "You'd think we'd have another gang of them knocking on our doors by now. But it's just been… quiet. It's bugging me out."

"Maybe it's something to do with what Mr. Kessler stole?"

Drew looked over. "What?"

"Andy's dad, Mr. Kessler. The girl said he stole something from The Order."

"He stole something? What was it?"

"We don't know yet. The girl just said they were looking for something he took last fall."

"Last fall's when everything went down with Andy. You think it could be connected?"

"Maybe, but...we don't know for sure. Andy's still trying to figure it out."

Drew scowled. "Great, so, Human kid, Andy's screwed up somehow and The Order might be comin' back. Anything else I should know?"

"I'm sorry," Cici's antennae drooped. "I didn't mean to like, bring you down or anything. I don't think we should worry about it too much. We've dealt with The Order before, haven't we?"

"Barely. We got lucky last time. If they come back in full force—"

Cici put her hands up. "Time out on that. Let's try to focus on the festival today, alright?"

"But—"

"I don't wanna talk about it anymore, man."

"Alright."

Drew took another puff of his cigarette, brow crunched in deep thought. Once he'd finished, he threw the butt into an empty can. Cici continued to fidget uncomfortably, clearly regretting having brought up anything. Drew felt bad.

"So...the festival," he said, clearing his throat. "What time are you heading out? I've got to be on stage by four."

Cici snapped her fingers a few times, trying to jog her memory. "Uh, yeah, right, I think I was gonna be meeting Andy at noon."

Drew glanced over at the digital clock on the oven.

"It's 11:50 right now."

"Aw, crap, really?!"

"If you need to get going, you can. I've got some stuff I've got to do yet. I'll see you guys in like…two hours. Let's meet at the Gravitron."

"Two o'clock at the Gravitron, got it," Cici bundled up her bag of jerky and headed toward the door, leaving her backpack on the ground beside Drew's couch.

"Hey, Ci? Your bag?"

"Just leave it," Cici called back as she rushed out the door and down the hall. "I wanna show you something later!"

Drew sighed, shoulders slumping, shaking his head as he walked over to close the door.

That kid was full of energy, he thought. *Too much.* He wasn't sure if it was the girl or just him, but either way, he found himself exhausted after every encounter.

Drew shuffled into the bathroom, squinting under the fluorescent lights. He pulled open the drawer beneath the sink, rummaging through a few old tubes of toothpaste and some floss picks until he found what he was looking for—a cheap makeup kit he'd picked up earlier in the week.

Popping open the plastic case, Drew examined the colorful assortment of whites, blacks and occasional grays that filled the tin. He dipped his fingers into the white and smeared it across his face, covering every inch of skin.

With careful strokes, Drew surrounded his eyes in black, extending the lines down his cheeks like inky tears. He did the same for his lips, drawing a ghoulish, cracked smile from cheek to cheek.

Drew stepped back to look himself over. This style seemed to work. He struck a few brooding poses, tilting his head this way and that. A small grin spread on his face as he admired the transformation.

The only problem now was his vibrantly colored hair—it threw off the whole look. He thought maybe he could hit up the apothecary for some sort of appearance-shifting potion, but with the side effects those tended to bring, plus the costs, he wondered if it was even worth it.

Suppose he had some time to explore his options. A quick trip through town wouldn't hurt.

Drew made his way out the front door. The narrow corridor ahead buzzed as always, once-white walls now a dingy yellow after years of neglect. The overhead lights cast a nauseating glow. The faded carpet beneath his shoes was worn thin in several spots, revealing patches of concrete and nail-filled wooden strips.

He strode down a few steps and around the crooked corners of the apartment, passing by his neighbors along the way. He could hear a few muffled arguments and blaring televisions. The air reeked of the diner below.

One last turn, and Drew was up against a heavy door, one which led to Yellow Devil's Dive. The perfect spot for a 'slice of nostalgia,' so long as you were born in the 1950s. Chrome, neon, polished red vinyl, it all made up for the look of the place, accompanied in large part by the old tunes being belted by the jukebox.

Along one wall, a row of plush booths invited patrons to take a seat—taking up one of these booths was Drew's landlord, and proprietor of the restaurant, a stout Kobold, Geb Fizetti. Sitting across, scribbling away in his notepad, was Vick. The Vampire was dressed up in a bisected suit, the left half white, the other half black. The makeup he wore reflected this, as grotesque, Grim-like cosmetics were only applied to the left hand side of his face.

"Two-Face, right?" Drew asked. Vick stopped talking for a moment and turned, not looking too surprised to see him.

"Oh, yeah," Vick threw up his arms a bit and pivoted to show off his look. "Do you dig it?"

"Yeah man. Straight up. Looks nice."

"Hey, Warren," Geb said, his scaly snout turning up at the man. "Vick and I were just talking about the new building."

46

"Right. Remember getting a notice about that. It's gonna suck, not waking up to your cooking every morning."

"You're always welcome at the new location. Just, ah—no smoking."

"Right. New owners are probably gonna put the kibosh on that."

"They're gonna do more than that," Vick set his notebook down. "Word is, they're gonna be doing some serious renovations with the building."

"Seriously?" Drew said.

Geb nodded. "It's gotten real bad, especially with our pest problem."

"Pest problem?" Drew shook his head. "I haven't seen any pests."

"Hoh, I can promise you bud, it's only a matter of time. Kloons, dozens of 'em, they've been showin' up everywhere! On my counters, in my toilets—I saw one of 'em bite a customer just this morning! You must've heard the shrieking."

As Vick jotted that detail down, Drew twisted a finger in his ear, trying to jog his memory. Nothing really came up, nothing beyond Cici's incessant rambling while they cleaned. He must have zoned out pretty hard.

"Kloons? Is it that time again?"

"Every 27 months." Vick said matter-of-factly. Drew groaned.

"Great. Just what we needed." Drew slid into the booth next to Vick. "So, what're they gonna do about 'em?"

"Not much we can do about the kloons right now...my suggestion? Board up your cracks. As for renovations, the new owners wanna 'modernize' the place." Geb made air quotes with his claws. "Talking about tearing down walls, redoing the wiring, maybe even adding another floor."

"Another floor?" Drew squinted, then fell back in his seat a bit. "Ain't that gonna force everybody out?"

"Yeah..." Geb grimaced. "Everybody's gonna have to relocate while they do the work. That includes you, Warren."

Drew's hands ran through his hair.

"Damn…where am I supposed to go?"

"I'm sure we can find you a place." Vick said. "Maybe you could crash with Andy for a bit? He could definitely use an adult right about now."

Drew raised an eyebrow. "Hey, kid? Aren't you supposed to be meeting him right about now?"

Vick checked his Batman watch and cussed underneath his breath. He slid past Drew, bony hip smacking Drew in the face. The man rubbed his nose, scowling at the Vampire as he scrambled.

"Sorry, gotta run," Vick called over his shoulder. "See you at the festival later!"

The store bell jingled to signal his exit, leaving Drew alone with Geb. The Kobold eyed his face paint with some amusement.

"Nice look you're rocking. Going for the hungover clown vibe?"

"Screw you," Drew grabbed a napkin from the table's dispenser and started dabbing away at the bits of makeup that felt smudged.

"Level with me. How long do I have before I need to clear out?"

Geb's scaly nostrils flared with a small huff. "A couple weeks, maybe a month tops. I know it's not ideal…"

"Not ideal?" Drew scoffed. "Dude, this sucks."

"I don't know, Warren. I only sent you around a dozen notices."

Drew about rested his face in his hands, stopping himself just short of ruining the rest of his makeup.

"I know, I know…I guess I didn't think it would actually happen, you know?"

Geb's face softened. "Look, I get it. Change is hard. But maybe this could be good for you. A fresh start, you know?"

"Yeah, right. A fresh start, here? Man, I've got nowhere to go. There's not one person here that trusts me."

"I trust you, Drew. Your band members, they trust you. Cici seems to trust you a heckuva lot. You've got options here, they're limited, but you've got a way out of this. Maybe you could talk with Mr. Hudson about getting your own place? Or like Vick said, see if Andy needs a roommate for a while?"

Drew shuddered. "Living with teenagers is a hard pass."

Geb shrugged. "Suit yourself, but you're gonna have to figure out something soon."

"Yeah, I know. I'll…think of something."

An awkward silence fell between the two of them. Geb went ahead and got up, shuffling over toward the counter to grab a fresh mug.

"Big show today, huh, Drew? Need a little pick-me-up before you go?"

Drew shook his head and stood up, scooting off his seat. "Nah, I'm good. I have enough anxiety as it is."

He pushed open the diner door, the little bell jingling overhead, and stepped onto the sidewalk. The brisk air swirled on by, waking him up a bit. Leaves crunched underneath his cleats, Drew starting down the street toward the park.

Hudsonville was buzzing with excitement. Storefronts were decked out in orange and black streamers, fake cobwebs and plenty of jack-o'-lanterns. A few rat-tailed children ran past Drew's feet, brandishing plastic swords.

He wondered more and more if his little performance was really going to be accepted by the general audience. It loomed like a dark cloud overhead. A knot tightened in his stomach. He'd been waiting years for this chance, but now that it was here, now the doubt began to creep in. The weight of expectation felt crushing.

The renovation news didn't help things either. While the town was known for its hospitality, there wasn't much of a hand of grace being extended to the likes of him.

Someone who got dozens killed.

Before he could finish dwelling on his thoughts, Drew stepped in something. He looked down to see a mouse-sized kloon, its candy guts spilling out from its side. It gave a defeated wheeze.

Drew recoiled in disgust. The kloon laid there, pathetically, its red nose twitching, its neon fur matted with dirt. The sidewalk was stuck with crushed caramel rolls and wrapped taffies imprinted with the underside of Drew's shoe.

For a brief moment, he felt a pang of sympathy for the creature. The sympathy quickly passed as Drew remembered Geb's words.

The kloon's oversized feet flopped uselessly as it tried to right itself. Its permanent grin seemed to mock Drew, even in its current state. This pest, this clown of a rat was all-but-responsible for suddenly upending his life. Maybe this one's untimely demise was just a bit of karmic justice.

It let out another weak honk, candy oozing from its ruptured side.

Drew shook his head and stepped over it, continuing on his way.

Good riddance.

CHAPTER 5

Among the first lodges to be constructed for the town back in the '80s was Andy's temporary home.

It once belonged to the mayor, Solomon J. Hudson—small, cozy, with a few throw rugs on the floor underneath its elongated furniture. Otto, a plump grey cat, sat stretched out in front of a window. Andy had picked him off the streets early on during his time here, right after Cici had threatened to eat the poor thing.

At the center of the living room, standing a few feet away from a buzzing television, Elena was surrounded by brushes.

"Hold still," Andy murmured, brow wrought in concentration as he applied a layer of sickly blue to the girl's cheeks. Elena squirmed in her spot, barely containing her enthusiasm.

"This is going to look so cool!" she giggled, turning her other cheek.

Cici's four arms worked in coordination as she styled Elena's hair into an elaborate updo. She laughed at the girl's comments, especially seeing how much they got to Vick; *that* teen sat on the saggy couch nearby, arms crossed over his chest, his nose wrinkled.

"What's with the look?" Cici asked.

"Don't think I need to tell you why this feels wrong." Vick groaned.

"I don't see you comin' up with anythin' better." Andy said. "Just make sure you keep your end of the illusion up."

"Yeah, yeah." Vick said as he sat up. "You about ready?"

"Just one last touch," Andy said as he applied some eyeliner. Cici tilted her head.

"Yo, Andy? Where did you learn to do all this?"

"Oh, hah…well, I was actually in a few stage plays, back home."

"You? In a stage play?" Cici shook her head. "I can't imagine."

"Not really on the stage, no. We didn't have lots of kids at the school that were into theater, so they had to make do with pretty much anybody who was interested. I liked to work on the sets, and I already knew a few of the guys from my guitar class."

Andy blinked. He wondered how those fellas were doing now. He wondered if they thought he was dead, or if he moved, or what. He wondered a lot about what the outside world was doing without him.

As Andy wondered, Vick got up off the couch.

"Alright, scoot over."

The Vampire formed a dark energy in between his hands, muttering old words beneath his breath. The energy coalesced into an orb of smoky shadows. With a final word, Vick clapped his hands together. Darkness cascaded over Elena, a blanket of black. Shadow particles drifted around her like confetti, settling onto the girl's head and washing her over in illusory ripples.

Elena giggled and twirled, arms outstretched. The dark motes clung to her hair, making it absorb the surrounding light. Her skin took on an eerily pale cast, the makeup Andy had so carefully applied blending seamlessly with magic to create a visage of bloodless pallor. The girl's eyes shifted from their vibrant greens to a bright crimson, her sclera growing as black as the night.

Vick took a moment to admire his handiwork.

"How's that?" he asked the others. They all nodded to one another.

"Pretty good. Just uh—one more thing," Andy walked over to the kitchen table and picked up a dark paper crown. He brought it over to Elena and set it upon her head. "There we go."

"Oh, oh! Can I see?" Elena quickly hobbled over to the bathroom to peep at herself in the mirror. Vick followed.

There was no reflection to be had, naught but the paper crown which adorned her head and the clothes that draped her body. Elena squealed with delight.

"You like it?" Vick asked.

"It's perfect!" Elena said.

"Sweet. Alright, just remember, you have to stay within ten meters of me at *all times*. The spell won't work if you don't."

"Gotcha!" Elena responded, running back out into the living room. Vick's eyes widened. He made sure to keep within range.

Cici passed both of them on her way to the bathroom, hoisting a big bag over her shoulder.

"I'm gonna get into my costume, then we can do pictures, alright?"

"How are you gonna take *my* picture?" Elena asked.

Vick winked. "Magic camera." As if that explained it. Elena seemed satisfied. Andy was not, but he wouldn't voice it. He was preoccupied already with putting the finishing touches on his own costume.

A white sweater, white pants and white shoes, all adorned with a white paper crown to contradict Elena's darker apparel. He had just finished taping the crown together, placing it now ever so delicately on top of his pompadour.

"So what are you guys supposed to be?" Vick asked as he got his camera ready.

"Like…chess pieces." Andy replied.

"Chess pieces?" Vick scoffed. "Like…what, the king and the queen?"

"Yeah."

"Chess. You're doing chess? You dork."

"What's wrong with chess?"

"Nothing's wrong with chess, just like. *Wow.* That's a pick."

"Let's see you come up with somethin' last second, pal. Elena wanted to do matching costumes. I was gonna be Elvis."

"I know, but chess? You couldn't have even tried to do like, Mario and Luigi? Or, or peanut butter and jelly?"

"What are you talking about?"

"I'm saying that of all the costumes you could have done, in *greyface*, no less—"

"Oh, boys!" Cici called in a sing-song voice from the other room. Andy and Vick turned.

Cici came out in a blur of jingling bells. Her square-patterned costume mixed obnoxious reds and nauseous blues.

The Xita had transformed herself into the spitting image of a medieval court jester, complete with an oversized hat adorned with long, floppy points that each ended in a tiny golden bell. With every movement, the hat chimed merrily. Even her antennae had been decorated in pom-poms.

"Ta-da!" Cici breathlessly struck a pose. "What do you guys think?"

Andy gave a polite clap, though it faded once he realized nobody would be joining him. Vick shook his head.

Cici looked a bit disappointed. "What? It's Pelé. Pelé the Clown? Pelé's Amazing Circus World?"

"Cici, nobody knows what that is." Vick said.

Tanya sheepishly raised her hand. Vick gawked. He almost completely forgot she was there, she was so quiet. Her over-the-top executioner's garb somehow didn't help her stand out.

"…Okay, so a few people know what that is." Vick said.

"Do you not like it?" Cici asked.

"No, I like it, it's just…Cici, with how you were talking it up, I was thinking it was gonna be something like…"

"Cooler?"

"More *iconic*." Vick said. "Like, somebody that *I* would know about."

"Well, Pelé's actually got a *huge* cult following, and—"

"Fellas," Andy clapped his hands a couple times to get their attention. "Runnin' a bit late already. Pictures, yeah?"

Vick nodded. He set his bulky Polaroid precariously on a stack of books which lay on the coffee table, trying to angle it just right.

"Everyone, over here." Vick said. "Stand together. Elena, you go in the front."

Andy helped guide everyone to their positions. Tanya silently took her place beside him and Elena. Cici bounced over, bells jingling with each step, and squeezed in close. As Vick lined up the shot, he put his hands out as if to say…

"*Stop!* There! Perfect. Okay, everyone on the count of five!"

Click.

The timer was set, and Vick rushed to join the rest.

"Cheese!" Cici and Elena shouted. Andy and Vick mumbled along.

The camera flashed, striking all with a momentary blindness. Vision clearing, Vick hurried over to retrieve the developing photo. Darkness gradually gave way to a charming scene of mismatched costumes and beaming faces. Like he promised, Elena's pale profile stood out front and center, ripe with excitement.

"I'd say that turned out pretty good." Vick said. The others gathered around him to get a better look.

"I love it!" Elena said. "Can I keep this?"

"We'll get a copy of it for you, sure." Vick said.

Cici leaned in. "Oh, look how cute we are! And Elena, you are *killing* it!"

Even Tanya, obscured by the darkness of her hood, gave a slight smile of the eyes.

Satisfied, the party gathered their things. Andy helped Elena into a small black cloak, while Cici adjusted her hat and boots one last time. Vick carefully packed away his camera equipment, and Tanya got back to sharpening her *very* real ax.

Cool air breezed past, stepping out of Andy's cabin. The lake shimmered nearby, its surface dotted in maple leaves. Their path was set—all they had to do now was walk it.

The closer they got to Hudsonville proper, the more festive the atmosphere became. Rustic decorations covered every home, the scent of cinnamon permeated the grounds. Colorful booths and tents lined the stony streets, each one offering games, food or goodie-bags of the Supernatural variety. A few small rides were set up, such as the spinning teacups and the kiddie-coaster. On the main stage, Hudson was playing a jaunty tune with his band. He could really tear it up on the saxophone.

It reminded Andy of all the times he and his mother would visit 'Riverpalooza' in Harpers Ferry. He thought about how they'd bring a bag lunch with their kayaks, munching on ham sandwiches while drifting down the river.

He missed those days. He missed his mother.

The group made their way through the bustling grounds, moving between tents and partygoers. Elena's eyes darted all over the place. She did her best to take in all the sights and sounds. It really was magical, all of it.

Cici's bells drew curious looks from a few passersby. Spinning around, she addressed the group while walking carelessly backwards.

"Okay, everyone! We should probably head to the Gravitron first!"

Andy listened with one ear, taking note of a booth selling caramel apples, a crowd quickly dispersing from it. Upon closer inspection, he could see several small creatures with bulbous noses scurrying between people's feet. They bit a few folks on the toes and were promptly kicked away.

"*Kloons*," Vick muttered, wrinkling his nose in disgust.

"Kloons?" Andy asked.

"Yeah, kloons. Pests. Guess you haven't really been around long enough to see a proper infestation yet."

They passed the Hall of Mirrors, where another commotion was brewing. A haggard-looking carnie was trying to shoo away a large group of the creatures that had somehow gotten inside. Their distorted reflections bounced between mirrors as they darted out, their warped, fake smiles boring into Andy's subconscious.

"They've been really bad this year, I guess," Vick said. "Fizetti's got to shut his current place down because of them."

"Dang, really?" Andy asked. "They don't look that terrible."

"They've got a pretty nasty bite," Vick grimaced.

As they neared the center of the festival grounds, the whirling lights and pulsing music of the Gravitron ride came into view. The large, wheel-shaped contraption spun around and around, pinning riders to its walls via centrifugal force.

Nearing the ride's entrance, Andy spotted a familiar figure leaning against the nearby lamp post. Drew stood, hands in his pockets, a cigarette dangling from his lips. The lights of the Gravitron occasionally illuminated his spooky makeup.

"There he is," Andy said, pointing.

Drew spotted the group approaching and flicked his cigarette to the ground. He pushed off from the post and approached.

"'Bout time you kids showed up," Drew grumbled, a hint of relief in his voice. His eyes landed on Elena. "So this is her?"

Andy scowled at Cici.

"You told him?"

"Well, yeah? Was I not supposed to?"

"No! This is—"

Drew put a hand up. "Chill out, little man. I'm not a snitch." He nodded at Elena. "Cool costume."

"Thanks!" she replied.

"Drew," Cici flourished her costume. "What do you think?"

"Nice. Jester. I like it." Drew said, nodding a few times.

"Well—it's not just a jester, it's like, supposed to be *Pelé*. Pelé the Clown?"

Drew did a double take of sorts, though he still wasn't drawing any connections from memory. Cici sighed.

"Forget it."

"What do y'all want to try first?" Andy asked, taking initiative.

"I know what I'm going for," Drew nodded toward the Gravitron. The line seemed to go on for a good few yards, but it was nothing too bad. Plus, the ride itself was usually over in under a minute.

The only one who lingered behind as the others got in line was Andy, as his stomach had never quite agreed with the spinning. He didn't mind staying back, however—there had been a big, fat, novelty turkey leg calling his name for some time now.

Over the course of the next two hours, the gang did their best to enjoy every attraction the festival had to offer. After the Gravitron, they made their way to the haunted hayride, where Elena clung to Tanya's arm.

Rather than last year's nondescript monster cutouts, many of which had been deemed offensive by the local homeowners association, this year the 'monsters' had been replaced with spooky knights. It seemed fear of The Natural Order was still fresh in everyone's minds.

The group tried their luck at various carnival games next. Cici's four arms gave her a slight one-up at the Hoop Shot. Overloading the system with three pointers, she won a humongous plush bat, which she immediately gifted to Elena. The girl hugged the soft toy close.

Everyone sampled an array of festival foods, from pumpkin-spiced funnel cake to caramel apples drizzled in chocolate. Vick got his long fangs stuck in one said apple—one of which had an artificial crown on it—so the group had to run his teeth under warm water until the sticky caramel came loose.

While the kids had their fun, Drew stuck around the beer tent for the most part, keeping an occasional eye on them when they trotted by. He just wanted to get his mind off the upcoming performance. Speaking of which, he hadn't even seen his bandmates yet.

What was taking them so long?

Walking past the petting zoo, Elena tugged on Andy's sleeve.

"Can we go see the animals?" she asked. Andy grinned from ear to ear.

"Yeah! Let's do it!"

Several pens lined with hay and mulch were open for any child to blindly wander into. Luckily for them, these were domesticated beasts with good manners.

Miniature drakes huffed small puffs of smoke, a group of fluffy jackalopes hopped about their enclosure. Andy was drawn to the bolter pens near the river, where a group of the giants were docked. Vick and Elena visited the perytons in the meantime. Elena giggled as she scratched at their feathery manes.

After spending some time among the critters, Drew found the group all crowded around a pile of sleeping drakes. He whistled to them.

"Hey! Almost showtime. You kids coming?"

Andy looked almost offended that Drew would wake these blissful, sleeping things. However, it appeared they had more to do yet. Everyone washed their hands and got moving.

The sky's bright blues had softened, the afternoon sun relaxing as it lazily approached the horizon. Drew checked his pocket watch, his face paling beneath the white makeup.

Deep breaths.

The group approached the main stage, where another dense crowd had already gathered. Mr. Hudson's band was finishing up their set, the last notes drawing out for dramatic effect. Drew headed toward the backstage. A few security guards stood up to check him in.

Cici gave Drew a tight hug. "You're gonna do great!"

Vick clapped Drew on the back. "Knock 'em dead, man."

Even Elena piped up with a "Good luck!"

Andy and Tanya stayed quiet, the both of them giving a thumbs up.

Drew gave Cici one last pat on the arm before heading up. Once he disappeared backstage, the rest of the kids made their way into the crowd to find seats. The festival grounds had transformed into a sea of eager Supernaturals. Twinkling lights criss-crossed overhead. The energy was electric.

Andy and Vick helped Elena through the throng of monsters, the rest bouncing behind them. Finally reaching some miraculously empty chairs, the group settled in. Andy helped make sure Elena was comfortable. Vick plopped down next to them, then Tanya, then Cici at the very end of the row.

The stage lights dimmed. A hush fell over the crowd as fog began to billow from all sides of the stage.

But nothing came. Nobody stepped out to greet them.

There was a moment where it seemed like everyone had been left waiting for a bit too long. *Where was the band?* The crowd murmured and murmured, until…

There, a lone figure emerged. Drew walked into the spotlight, gripping his guitar tightly, sweat dripping down his temples.

"Hey, ladies and gents," Drew's shaky voice seeped through the speakers. "I uh…hate to be the bearer of bad news, but…it doesn't look like Acid Age is gonna be joining us tonight."

A collective groan rippled through the audience. Cici's face fell.

"But," Drew continued, taking in a deep breath. "But…*I'm* still here. And I very much *plan* on giving the people *exactly what they want.*"

The crowd broke into a cautious cheer, the disappointment of a moment ago *nearly* forgotten. Still, there was palpable tension in the room as to whether or not he'd pull it off.

Drew strummed his guitar once. A crow of metal echoed throughout the fairgrounds. The crowd grew silent, and Drew began to work his magic.

His fingers danced across the fretboard, launching into a blazing riff. The crowd bobbed their heads to the rhythm.

As he transitioned into the chorus, fingers shredding the strings, a rumble built beneath the crowd's feet. It was hardly noticeable at first. Quiet, low, but beginning to grow. Plastic cups rattled on tables. The streamers overhead suspiciously swayed. A few audience members exchanged worried glances, but most thought it was all part of the show.

Lost in the music, Drew played on.

But a violent tremor rocked the festival grounds. Several stumbled, struggling to keep their balance. Elena clung to Andy's arm, squealing. The music screeched to a halt. Drew grabbed the microphone stand to steady himself.

"What the hell?" he said, the words echoing. A still silence followed for but a moment.

Another powerful quake shook the earth. Screams erupted from the crowd as everyone scrambled to evacuate. Tents collapsed, rides groaned.

"Everyone stay calm," Hudson's megaphone-amplified voice boomed above the chaos. "Please exit the festival grounds in an orderly fashion!"

But his words were eventually drowned in shrieks.

Tanya scooped Elena up in her arms, Andy close behind. Vick and Cici pushed through the crowd, trying to clear a path.

As they neared the closest clearing, a deafening crack split the air. The ground beneath their feet fractured. Fissures snaked across the cobblestone, widening into gaping chasms.

From those chasms, a sea of red noses and painted faces emerged from the depths. Thousands upon thousands of kloons poured forth, their fluffy, multi-colored bodies bouncing up and down, their grins wide. The tiny creatures swarmed over everything in their path, a living tide of vicious piñatas.

Andy watched on as the horde engulfed people left and right. Cici shrieked as a mass of the things latched onto her costume, dragging her down into the writhing sea of fur. Vick cried out, reaching for her, though another surge of kloons knocked him off balance, sweeping him away in the same direction. Before he could mouth a single spell, his voice was muffled by the fluff.

Tanya fought valiantly to clear a path, but there were simply too many. The kloons swarmed up her legs, weighing her down. With a growl of frustration, she toppled backwards into the surging mass, Elena going with her.

Andy shouted as he reached for Elena's hand. He latched on, determined not to lose her too. The girl trembled, tears streaming down her cheeks.

"Help me," she whimpered. A few of the things crawled across her face.

"I've got you!" Andy said. He pulled with all his might, Elena just about breaking free from the kloons' grip. Just then, a particularly large surge of them slammed into the boy's legs. Andy stumbled, his grip on Elena's hand loosening. Their fingers slipped apart.

Elena screamed as the kloon tide swallowed her whole.

Andy attempted to lunge, but he was already being dragged away. He caught one last glimpse of Elena's flailing arms before she and Tanya vanished into the nearby fissure.

All his friends, gone in an instant, drowned along with the center stage. And Elena—he promised to keep her safe.

He failed her.

The kloons surged at Andy's sides, threatening to drag him under as well. A fire ignited in his chest. Adrenaline surged through his veins. His pupils flashed. Claws extended from his fingertips.

Andy swung wildly, swatting away small swaths of the creatures. His superhuman strength sent them flying, squeaky honks cut short as they slammed into nearby booths. Fading fast, Andy could still make out Elena's scent. He charged forward, plowing through the writhing mass of grinning faces. Kloons crunched and popped beneath his feet. His claws tore through any creatures that dared cling to him.

Andy skidded to a halt at the edge of the yawning fissure, peering down into the darkness. The stench of something sweetly rotten assaulted him from below.

Without hesitation, he crouched down, calves coiling like springs.

"I'm comin', fellas!"

Andy dove into the chasm, plummeting head-first into the dark.

CHAPTER 6

The air whipped past, the dark all-consuming. Andy's limited vision caught flashes of blood-red *something* growing from the cavern walls. He reached out to one to try and stop himself, breaking his fall before he could approach deadly velocity.

Of course, the moment he gripped the mushroom's soft edges, it violently tore, leaving Andy dangling by a thread of mycelium before he dropped again.

He could still just barely catch a whiff of his friends. Plummeting, Andy punched off the wall to propel himself toward the scent.

The mushrooms thankfully helped soften each impact with the walls, their numbers growing larger the deeper he descended. Andy bounced from shroom to shroom all the way down, though the bottom came a lot later than he first anticipated.

Seconds stretched to minutes as he spiraled endlessly downward. The walls began to grow further and further apart, Andy's safety net being dragged away along with them. A creeping dread took hold. *How far down did this chasm go? Would he ever reach the bottom? And this was assuming the bottom was something soft…*

Panic set in. Andy screamed, helplessly swinging his limbs. The walls were gone, the darkness pressed in on all sides. He tried to grab onto something, anything, to slow his descent, but there was nothing to grasp within the endless void.

Just as he had resigned himself to a messy fate, a massive shape peered out from the darkness. His eyes widened as he made out the colossal cap of a mighty mushroom, easily the size of a stadium. Andy slammed into the enormous fungus with bone-jarring force. The impact knocked the wind out of him, though the rubbery flesh absorbed most of the blow. He bounced high into the air, tumbling head over heels.

Up and down, each rebound sent him a little lower than before. His stomach lurched with each rise as he struggled to regain his bearings. After a painful few seconds as a paddle ball, the boy's momentum petered out. He came to rest face down on the spongy surface, panting.

Heart pounding, lungs heaving, he tried to catch his breath. Cammy flesh expanded and contracted beneath him. A faint glow was visible just up ahead, as some bioluminescent blue protrusions lined the grounds around the enormous amanita.

Groaning, the boy pushed himself up onto his hands and knees. His white costume was soaked in streaks of blue juice. No longer in shock, Andy could hear the distant honking of kloons, and the rhythmic dripping of water. The air down here was thick, damp, and full of decay.

One smell cut above the rest.

Elena's.

Andy's nostrils flared. He inhaled deeply, picking up on a few more traces—Vick's cologne, Cici's slightly bitter scent, Tanya's earthy musk.

There was something else too, an acrid smell that made his nose shrivel—burnt hair mixed with a sickly sweet. Andy crawled to the edge of the giant cap, peering down at the cavern floor. In the dim light, he could make out a trail of sizzling corpses, tiny pools of liquefied caramel oozing from the fell kloons' ruptured bodies.

His eyes followed the trail, noting the tell-tale signs of a struggle. Deep claw marks gouged the earth, crushed fluff spattered against the rocks, bits of Cici's costume clinging to a few odd stalagmites.

Hundreds of seemingly unharmed paw prints were embedded into the mud as well. Andy growled. *Those* tracks led further in.

Elena's crown rested on the damp floor, surrounded by sizzling fur. Andy's heart sank when it passed his vision. He leapt down, landing with a soft thud. Carefully, he picked up the crown, turning it over in his hands. The delicate paper was crumpled and torn, stained in mushroom juice and smudged makeup. Andy's chest tightened.

She was so excited to go to this festival.

He was about to tuck the crown into his pocket when a blood-curdling scream echoed through the cavern.

"Cici!" Andy cried.

Without a moment's hesitation, the boy took off running in the direction of the scream. His shoes slapped against the damp stone, following the trail. The scent grew stronger and stronger.

A chorus of screams accompanied, echoing throughout the tunnel. It was disorienting, confusing—Andy gripped his sensitive ears tight and picked up his pace. The cries came from all directions at once, bouncing off the curved walls, amplifying into a deafening screech.

His eyes darted from corner to corner, searching for any sign of Cici, but she was nowhere to be seen.

No matter. Andy was intent on following the trail, and on getting away from these screams. The passage was hardly illuminated beyond the soft glow of his eyes. Andy had to rely on his other senses to get him through.

A pit grew in his stomach. *Just how deep were these caverns? Realistically, how was he going to get out of here?* He didn't really come with much of a game plan at all, now that he thought about it.

Was he stupid?

There was no use beating himself up about it, now. His friends, they had to be up ahead. Surely they would do the ridiculing for him.

The ground beneath Andy's feet became increasingly wet with each step. Tendrils of pale mycelium crept across the tunnel's floors and walls, weaving into a thickening carpet of slimy skin.

Andy found himself surrounded by grotesque fungus. Enormous mushrooms of various hues sprouted from every surface, caps glistening in the low light. Shelf fungi jutted out from the walls in tiered formations, luminescent spores floating lazily through the air around them.

The entire chamber pulsed with lichen, quivering, undulating as if reacting to his presence. As Andy's eyes adjusted, he noticed something large and reflective embedded in the far wall; an eye staring back at him—Cici's. The girl gasped.

"Is someone there?" Cici asked, her voice full of phlegm. "Can you please help?"

"Cici, it's me," Andy said, approaching. He tugged at the fibrous growths that held Cici in place, his claws sinking into the fungal flesh with ease. "I'm gonna get you out of here, okay? Just hang tight."

"Andy? Aw, man, they got you too?"

"I'm alright. Just came down here to get you guys."

"Gee, that's nice of you," Cici coughed a few times.

"Do you know where the others got took?"

Cici shook her head as much as she could while restrained. "Vick was able to fight off the kloons for the most part. We got away from them for a little bit, but then we got ambushed," Cici grimaced. "Some…jerk with a club for an arm."

"A club for an arm?"

"Yeah—a Mycarnid, I think."

Andy's brows furrowed. Mycarnids were a strange case, from his experience. Amicable, community-driven, they were people, for sure, but…*very* primitive ones. They were easily angered, quite violent and feral when their peace felt threatened.

That's why it was all-the-stranger to find Cici in one piece. The Mycarnids Andy was familiar with would have ripped her to shreds by now. The idea that one would go out of their way to merely incapacitate her and hang her up like a wall ornament, it didn't sit right.

As the last entrapping tendrils fell away, Cici stumbled into Andy's arms, sputtering.

"Easy, there." Andy said. "Can you walk?"

"Yeah. I think so. Just give me a sec." Cici said.

Andy helped her regain her balance, watching as she took a few careful test steps. Her jester costume was tattered, a singular bell hanging limply from what remained of her hat. Despite her condition, her eye still held that usual spark. A quick breath out, and Cici was standing back up straight again.

"Let's go find everyone!" Cici said.

They turned toward the tunnel Andy came from, ready to retrace his steps. As the kids approached the entrance, however, the both of them froze up.

There, floating in the miasma, a cluster of moist, beady eyes stared back at them. From the dark emerged the offending Mycarnid, draped in a dirty ragged cloak. His body was an expected amalgamation of fungal growths and recycled bones. Thick tendrils of lichen writhed like large veins spread across his body, the stretched tissue struggling to hold the creature together.

His head was bloated, a large cap with dozens of bulging eyes, each studying the children with intent. Below his cap was a grotesque maw, rows of banana-shaped teeth lining the inside. Drool slowly dripped from his gnashing jaws.

The creature narrowed his many eyes. From beneath his cloak, he revealed his large, swollen, club-like limb. Without taking his eyes off the creature, Andy reached back and gently pushed Cici behind him.

"How do you wanna do this?" Andy whispered.

"He probably knows where the others are," Cici said. "Maybe we can do a little 'convincing' on our end."

"Guess it's worth a shot. Can you distract him?"

Nodding, Cici scooped up a small handful of mushrooms from the ground. The Mycarnid turned toward her and hissed.

"H-hey, big guy," she called, taking a few steps backward. "You wanna see a magic trick?"

The Mycarnid paused. Cici took a deep breath, hiding the mushrooms behind her back. Now was her time to shine.

"Okay, watch closely!" She held up her hands, exposing her palms to the creature. Empty. The creature's eyes blinked out of sync with one another, each fixated on a different movement. Cici's hands went back into hiding, and one by one, she picked out a juicy fungus in each.

The Mycarnid squinted his eyes and took another step toward Cici—exactly when she began to juggle. Four hands worked in perfect coordination, tossing the fungi around in intricate patterns.

The Mycarnid was not impressed. He continued approaching.

"Aw, what, you didn't like it?" Cici asked.

Thud, thud, thud—that was a step too close for the girl.

She tossed her handful of fungus into the creature's face and bolted in the opposite direction. Along the way, she was sure to pluck each and every mushroom that graced her path. The Mycarnid roared and made chase.

As that happened, Andy focused on achieving his usual metamorphosis; His eyes clenched tight, an inner fire ignited in his chest. A familiar, primal feeling threatened to bubble over.

He doubled over, his tendons twitching, his muscles swelling beneath his skin. His bones snapped, retracting and reforming as his frame expanded. Coarse, brown bristles sprouted across his arms, his face—his whole body was rapidly engulfed in itchy fur.

His face extended forward, his teeth sharpening into fierce points. His eyes blazed with intense light, a black mask of fur forming around them.

From the veil of his pained roars, there emerged a hearty and satisfied laughter.

Rex was free.

Across the chamber, Cici, cornered, scrambled up the slimy wall. Her fingers dug into its uneven surface. The Mycarnid swiped at her with his club-like arm, the appendage whistling through the air, inches away from hitting its mark.

Realizing his quarry was out of reach, the Mycarnid turned, ready to go after his other prey—but instead of the unassuming chubby kid that had once occupied the space, there was...*that*, a giant brick wall of fur and meat. The Werewolf towered, even over the Mycarnid, a wide grin plastered on his canine face.

"Heya, bub," Rex greeted as he cracked his knuckles.

The Werewolf threw a big right hook, the Mycarnid clocked hard. He retaliated with a swing of his engorged limb overhead. Rex caught the blow on his forearm, the impact sending shockwaves through his body. He grunted but held his ground, using his superior strength to push back. The two behemoths shuffled toward the wall.

With a swift motion, Rex reached out, his large hands encircling the Mycarnid's thick neck. The creature squirmed, but there was no breaking free of the Werewolf's iron grasp. Battle cries descended into gasps. He clawed desperately at Rex's arm with his webbed hand.

Rex boomed with laughter, echoing throughout the chamber. With a heave, he lifted the Mycarnid off his feet and chucked him like a ragdoll. The creature hurled through the air before crashing through a thin wall of mycelium. A cloud of spores erupted upon impact.

"C'mon, Bug-Eyes!" Rex said. "Is that all you got?"

He approached the fallen Mycarnid, teeth bared. The creature stayed put, an apparent gesture of surrender. But, just as his victory seemed assured, the Mycarnid lunged forward, extending his claws toward Rex's chest. Too swift of a movement—Rex couldn't juke this one. The claws cut deep. Blood trickled down Rex's ginger fur.

He staggered backward as his hand clamped the wound. Strange blisters rapidly formed underneath. They pulsed and throbbed, as if they had a life of their own. Before he could really react, the blisters burst, one after another, soft caps rapidly growing across Rex's chest.

He grunted, frantically trying to rip the things out. Each mushroom he pulled revealed two more growing in its place. A cold dread crept down his spine. He was quickly being overrun with fungus.

As he was distracted, the Mycarnid lunged again. With a crazed rasp, he swung his club-arm this time, sending the Werewolf flying across the chamber. Luckily, Rex landed on top of a cushy bed of caps. Unluckily, the veiny mycelium began to stretch over him, believing him to be one of their own. Rex writhed as he was pulled further in.

The Mycarnid approached, cackling as he readied to swing his arm once more. Like a cruel game of whack-a-mole, he brought the club down onto the prone wolf, driving him deeper and deeper into the ground. Before he could beat Rex into any more of a pulp, however, something jingled from up above—Cici, the muddy jester, landed directly on the Mycarnid's back. She pummeled him, her armored fists landing with satisfying thumps against his bulging eyes.

The Mycarnid roared and bucked, trying to throw his unexpected visitor off his shoulders, but Cici held fast.

She had to buy the big guy some time.

Catching hold of one of the clustered eyes, Cici twisted hard. The Mycarnid yowled as a gush of blue liquid spurted from the socket. Enraged, he finally managed to toss Cici away. She crashed hard into the ground.

The Mycarnid hissed, charging. Cici woozily got to her feet, hardly prepared to meet him head on, when suddenly, he stopped—grabbed from behind.

Rex, having freed himself from the fungal trap, held the creature in place. Grabbing him by the sides, claws digging in deep, Rex leveraged his strength against the Mycarnid's bulk. The Werewolf pivoted and threw himself backward.

Cici gasped. *The fabled German suplex.*

The resulting impact shook the chamber. A cloud of dust erupted around them as their bodies came to a halt. Rex rose. His eyes scanned the fallen foe, checking him for any movement, making sure he was down for the count. Just to be sure, Rex placed one his foot on the Mycarnid's chest. The creature groaned beneath him, his eyes wincing all together now.

Rex grumbled, scratching at the fungus that continued to grow from his chest. It seemed to be slowing down at this point. That, and the creature's meek whimpers, indicated a truer form of surrender.

Cici dusted herself off, watching as Rex subdued their adversary. Besides the muck staining her costume, and some mild bruising on her exoskeleton, she appeared unharmed.

"Hey, big guy." Cici said. "You alright?"

Rex turned, giving a low grunt of affirmation. His gaze softened. "You?" he asked.

"Never better," Cici said with jazz hands. Rex snorted and turned his attention back to the whimpering creature pinned beneath him. He leaned in close, snout wrinkling as he took in his scent. The Mycarnid's eyes continued to dart around.

"Alright, bub. Where're you keepin' everyone else?" Rex asked.

The Mycanid hissed; Rex drove his heel further into the creature's 'ribs.'

"We can do this one bone at a time. Tell me what I wanna know."

The Mycarnid's eyes narrowed. Reluctant, he croaked a single word.

"*Below.*"

CHAPTER 7

Rex and Cici looked at each other, exchanging a waggle of brows. Rex pressed harder.

"Yeah? How do we get *below?*"

"Show you, if free Meat-Man." the creature croaked.

"Meat-Man?" Cici asked. "Is that your name?"

The Mycarnid nodded. Cici tugged on Rex's shorts.

"Why don't we let him go?" she said.

Rex growled, though looking at the helpless creature, he felt just a tiny twinge of pity. Maybe there was still a small part of Andy in there, pulling him back, keeping him from turning this jerkwad into mincemeat. Regardless, the Werewolf stepped off, massive shoulders sagging.

"Don't try nothin' funny, guy." Rex said. Cici laughed out loud, helping the creature to his feet. Meat-Man had to use his club-like appendage to steady himself, many of his bones broken over the course of his fight. Cici cringed as she watched, deciding to be a shoulder for the creature to lean on, despite what had just happened.

Meat-Man seemed to appreciate this, at least.

He led the group further into the chamber, further below. Rex scanned the darkness warily, claws at the ready. Cici continued to act as Meat-Man's crutch and moral support.

The gathered few clambered through a small hole in the ground, one at a time. It was thankfully just large enough for Rex to squeeze through.

Punctuated with countless more holes, the chamber below housed various huddled figures. Rex grit his teeth when he saw them—Vick and Tanya trapped in this grotesque nest, ensnared by Meat-Man's obsessive instinct. Fungal bodies fruited from various spots on their skin. It made the Werewolf furious.

"Let them go." Rex said firmly. Meat-Man recoiled, casting his multitude of bulging eyes at the shadows where his prisoners dwelled.

"Gifts from the sky," Meat-Man growled, shaking his head. "*Friends* for Meat-Man."

"You and me got *very* different definitions of *friends*. Let them go, now."

The creature flinched, approaching the cells where the kids were held captive. He drew his claws across the mycelium walls, setting free both children.

Vick's suit was expectedly tattered, dotted in rubbery growths. The black and white fabric was now marred with splotches of brown and blue. Blinking awake, the Vampire's gaze landed on Rex's towering form, himself yelping. As his rescuer's outdated hairdo came into focus, however, his expression eased considerably.

"Took you guys long enough." Vick said.

"Next time, cut *yourself* out," said Rex.

"I'm kidding," Vick put his hands up in surrender. "Thanks."

Tanya seemed to have lost her hood on the way down. Any mushrooms budding from her body were encased in a thick layer of protective amber, her syrupy blood acting as a natural defense mechanism. Once she stirred awake, she very thoroughly checked herself for her tools—her 'prop' ax was still thankfully dangling at her side. She gave a grateful look to Rex, turning aggressively toward Meat-Man. Cici took a quick step between the both of them.

"Woah, hey, we're like, chill now." Cici said. Tanya gave her a dismissive glance, continuing to stare the creature down. Meat-Man took a cautious step back, hissing quietly.

That was just about everyone accounted for. *Just about.* Rex's nose twitched as he searched for another scent. Though the brutish alter-ego had hardly the memory of the child, Andy's voice rang out clear in his head; he had to find Elena fast, or they'd both be in trouble.

His heart only sank when he couldn't pick up any trace of her.

"Where's the little girl?" he growled, turning to Meat-Man.

Meat-Man's many eyes blinked rapidly. "No little girl here."

Rex grabbed Meat-Man by his shoulders and hoisted him into the air—before he could rip the Mycarnid to shreds, though, Vick stepped up, placing a careful hand on the Werewolf's back.

"Woah, buddy! He's right. Elena's not here." Vick said.

Rex's eyes flickered toward Vick, still gripping Meat-Man as tight as a squeaky toy.

"What do you mean? Where is she?" he asked.

"When we fell, it was *chaos.*" Vick said. "Kloons everywhere, like a freaking tide of them. I started blasting them, but during all the mixup, there was just—there was no way to keep track of her, and she..." he paused, swallowing hard. "They took her deeper into the caves."

Rex's fur bristled. He slowly lowered Meat-Man to the ground, though his claws remained extended, twitching with barely contained rage. He paced back and forth, casting long, manic shadows. The others huddled together, faces etched with both anguish and relief. Tanya especially looked rather sour, though as always, she stayed her tongue on the matter.

The fur rapidly shed from the beast's body, his mass quickly drained. As his bones cracked and receded, and Andy toppled over, Vick was right there at his side to help keep him steady.

Cici surveyed the network of tunnels branching out before them. Each dark passage looked identical to the last, an endlessly dizzying maze of sloppy stone. She imagined Elena lost and alone in that sickening darkness, shuddering at the thought.

Vick ran a hand through his gunked-up hair.

"Gods, what do we do?" he asked. "These caves could go on for miles. We could search for days and never find her, *or* a way out."

"Don't say that." Cici said. "She can't be far off. Maybe we just need to follow where the kloons went."

"Are you *crazy?*" Vick hissed.

"I don't know," Cici said, arms dramatically thrown to her sides. "What else do we have to go off of? It's not like we know our way around down here."

"Meat-Man knows the way." the creature simply said. The others turned to look at him, then back at each other. Cici gave Vick a slow and sheepish shrug of her shoulders.

"No." Vick said. "We're not going with the monster man."

"Meat-Man!" the creature corrected.

"Come on, he said he was sorry." Cici said.

Andy coughed a few times, swallowing some residual bile.

"I don't think he did," he said, wiping the drool from his lips. "But it don't matter. If he can help us find Elena, we're going with him."

"You too?" Vick asked.

"He probably knows this place better than any of us. I say he's our best bet of making it out of here alive," An uncharacteristic, devilish grin spread on Andy's face. "And heck, if we get hungry, maybe we cook ourselves some mushroom stew."

Gulp. Meat-Man took another step back.

Tanya, lips pursed, gave a curt nod. Andy and Cici followed suit. Vick, outnumbered by his peers, massaged his temples.

"We're *screwed,*" he said.

"What Meat-Man get?" the creature asked.

Cici, as always, was delighted to take the opportunity.

"Well maybe we can all be friends," she offered.

Though Vick groaned at the thought of it, Meat-Man's eyes all lit up at once.

"*Friends* for Meat-Man?"

"Yeah," Cici said with a shrug. "I mean, that's what you wanted, right? Just don't like…put us in those hives again, okay? Or try and eat us."

A tempting offer. The Mycarnid scratched his chin and grumbled to himself.

"Follow."

"Alrighty," Andy said with a wave of his hand. "Lead the way, Mr. Man."

The group fell in line, Andy and Tanya bringing up the rear. The two were poised, ready to strike should their guide show the slightest hint of betrayal. Vick floated along, sandwiched in the middle of the group. Cici was the only one actively walking alongside Meat-Man. She kept him good company, going on and on about her mountains of movie knowledge.

The Mycarnid led the group through the maze, climbing over shelves of mycelium, checking behind his back every now and again to make sure everyone was keeping up.

Soon enough they found the massive cavern from whence they came. Andy recognized the colossal cap he had landed on earlier, its surface indented from everyone's fall. Still scattered around the floor were the charred remains of countless kloons.

Andy crouched down to examine one of the charred corpses, cringing at the smell. The once colorful fur was now blackened and crispy, wisps of smoke still curling from its singed remains.

Cici poked at another with a stick, causing part of its body to crumble away. She tried turning it over to see if there were any salvageable innards, but the candies, too, were far overcooked. An amalgamate ooze was sizzling out from the confines of their silvery wrappers. *Eugh.*

A pattern emerged, several creatures having run in a certain direction. A winding path of blackened bodies led toward one of the larger tunnels branching off from the hollow. Barely tangible in the musty air was Elena's ever-fleeting scent. Andy's eyes narrowed.

So far so good.

"Look here," the boy said, pointing toward the trail. "I think they took her this way."

Meat-Man swiveled to follow Andy's gesture. He let out a low, rumbling growl of acknowledgement before shuffling toward the opening, the others following.

A slight draft blew from within the passage itself. Sparse patches of bioluminescence hardly penetrated the darkness ahead.

Meat-Man halted, his head tilting from left to right. The group gathered around, all of them trying to get a glimpse at what was so interesting up ahead.

Remnants of something littered their oncoming path. Planks of wood, some still bearing traces of varnish, lay scattered across the ground. Twisted metal rods jutted out at odd angles, once-shiny surfaces now dulled by dust.

The debris grew more concentrated as they pressed onward. Fragments of what appeared to be sound equipment—a crushed speaker here, a tangle of frayed wires there—mingled with the rough terrain. A broken guitar sat propped precariously against the tunnel wall, polished surface reflecting the mushrooms' glow.

Tattered strips of fabric fluttered from the spiny stones up top. A faint breeze jostled them gently. They were banners, bearing the fall festival logo, its cheerful orange and black design smeared with cave grime. Just as she stepped forward to investigate, Meat-Man gripped her by the shoulder and forcibly pulled her back. The others were put on high alert, fists balling, but before they could teach the Mycarnid a lesson—

SMAAAASH!

…A massive stage light came crashing down right where Cici was about to step. It sent a shower of sparks and glass over everyone.

The girl stumbled backward, antennae quivering, her body otherwise stiff.

"Thanks." she mumbled. Meat-Man gave an affirmative nod. Cici gulped.

"Drew's gotta be down here, too, huh?"

"Maybe. We don't know yet." Andy said.

"I hope he isn't hurt."

"I'm sure even if he was, he'd be okay. Heck, he's probably looking for us right now."

"Yeah," Cici sniffled. "Right."

Andy gave her shoulder a reassuring squeeze before turning his attention back to their debris-strewn path. The group carefully picked their way through the wreckage, mindful now of any other precariously dangling equipment that threatened to come crashing down. Everyone did their best to efficiently duck the scaffolding and skirt around its fixtures.

There, a scent—a cheap scent, carcinogenic, festered in the air. Drew's scent, faint but unmistakable.

"Hold up," Andy said, raising a hand. He closed his eyes, focusing intently. The boy crouched down, running his fingers through the damp soil. As he sifted through the dirt, his hand brushed against something like paper, squishy; a used filter. It was still warm.

Crunch.

The sound of footsteps on broken glass echoed behind. Andy's ears pricked up.

A shadowy figure emerged from a fallen truss, brandishing what looked to be a large pipe. His ghostly face was barely illuminated in the dark.

"*Raaahhh!*"

The group scattered as the figure swung wildly, narrowly missing Vick's head. Cici shrieked and dove behind a pile of debris. Tanya rolled out of the way, Meat-Man lumbered backwards.

Andy stumbled onto his rear end, looking up in horror as the unfamiliar figure loomed above, his pipe raised high—but just as he was about to bring it down, the attacker froze.

"Andy?"

That voice made Andy do a double-take. The figure lowered the pipe, his face easier to make out now that it hadn't been in motion. Drew; so he *was* okay. Andy let out a soft breath of relief. Immediately following, Drew was tackled to the ground.

Tanya placed the man into a painful-looking arm bar, threatening to break it if he so much as moved an inch. The others were on top of Drew just as quickly, Cici kicking him while he was down, Meat-Man mimicking the same.

"Stop," Andy hollered. "It's just Drew!"

The others paused. Drew groaned, rolling onto his side and clutching his ribs. Despite taking a beating, he looked strangely satisfied.

"Alright. Yeah. Good on you." he wheezed. Drew got to his feet, reached out to Cici first, and pulled her in for a tight hug. He soon caught his breath and swallowed, letting the girl go. The look she saw on his face was...*mortifying.*

The absolute state of the children, their once-vibrant costumes now stained and ravaged. These kids—brave kids, foolish kids— they'd fallen right into this nightmare with him. They were stuck down here, stuck in this dank, treacherous maze, all because of him. *Him and his stupid performance.*

Drew's shaking fingers ran slowly through his hair, the man wincing as his claws caught onto a tangle.

"You shouldn't *be* down here," he said.

He scanned the group again, noticing for the first time that a head was missing.

"Where's the Human?"

The kids all exchanged a glance—their silence spoke for them.

"Oh, man," Drew massaged his eyes. His shoulders slumped.

"We don't know where she went," Andy said. He puffed his chest out a bit. "The kloons took her deeper into the caves. We're tryin' to find her."

"This is all my fault."

"It's not your fault, Drew." Cici said, reaching for his arm. "You couldn't have known this would happen."

Drew shook his head, unconvinced. Still, the show must go on.

"Right...We'll find her. And I'll get you all home. Promise."

"Meat-Man help too," the creature said. "Meat-Man knows the caves. Meat-Man show the way."

Drew had only now noticed the hulking figure that loomed behind the children. All he could manage at first was a squint, one that widened dramatically.

"*Meat-Man?*"

The kids looked at each other.

"You know this freak?" Vick asked.

"Of course I know him. Meat-Man and I are tight." Drew said.

"You're *tight?*" Vick said. "I'm pretty sure he just tried to *eat* us."

Drew glared at Meat-Man. The Mycarnid shook his head. "*No* true. Meat-Man stored friends for safe-keep."

"Is *that* what that was?" Andy asked.

"Can we go back for a sec?" said Cici. "How do you know Meat-Man?"

"Ehh? I mean, I kinda know *all* the Mycarnids. You remember when we first met?"

Andy could recall—Drew and Cici had devised a plan to help him escape the valley—that's when he found out about 'Mycopolis.' The initial experience was hardly pleasant, ending in a chase toward a bottomless pit.

Andy wondered for a moment if *this* was the same poor sod he'd shoved into said abyss. Information to keep to himself, for now. He would rather his only guide in these dark depths not be reminded of past transgressions.

"Yup." Andy said. "That probably could've gone better."

"No use sulking about it now," said Drew. "We've got a long climb ahead of us. Where are we going, Meat-Man?"

"City," Meat-Man said, nodding his head in the direction of the upcoming tunnels. "Meat-Man explored."

"A city?" Drew pursed his lips. It wasn't entirely out of the realm of possibility.

"If there's a city down here, what're you still doing all by yourself?" Vick asked.

"Nobody there," Meat-Man said. "Got scared."

Vick sighed. "*Great.*"

"Hey, it's something," Andy said, giving Vick a light tap on the arm. "A city's got to have access to the surface, I reckon."

"What makes you so sure?" Vick asked.

"I ain't. But we don't got many choices, now, do we?"

"Guess not."

"Right. So let's just see where this goes."

"Agreed," Drew said, giving Vick a pat on the back. Vick huffed and crossed his arms, resigning himself to the Mycarnid's guidance. The creature nodded, and continued through the dark.

While Cici chattered with Drew and Meat-Man, Andy found himself falling back to walk with Tanya and Vick. Sensing their irritation, he kept his mouth shut. Their footsteps were all that occasionally mingled with Cici's laughter up ahead.

There was a faint glow in the distance, a teal that flickered across the wet walls. The hour-long tunnel had suddenly opened into a vast expanse. Before them stretched a long bridge of an unknown element, its surface worn smooth by the passage of centuries. The bridge spanned a deep chasm with no end in sight. Its only respite from the dark were two blazing braziers lining the mouth of the cave. Their flames danced in a brilliant azure.

Their gazes were drawn upward. Their breathing unanimously hitched.

An entire city hung suspended from the rocky ceiling, its pyramids and spires pointing downward toward the abyss. The inverted metropolis was dizzying, its architecture alien. Ornate towers and domed structures clung to the cavern roof, glistening with precious metals. Delicate bridges and walkways connected the buildings, creating an Escher-esque web of pathways throughout. The sheer scale of it all was difficult to comprehend.

The city pulsated with a faint inner light, as if infused with something ancient, and mystical. Wisps of glowing spores drifted lazily around the inverted spires, like stars in the night sky.

A cool breeze wafted up from the depths, carrying with it the faint scent of something seductive. Soft susurrations of wind carried false voices and their long-lost hymnals.

Meat-Man cowered as he gazed toward the bottom. All it took was a good shove from the others to keep him going.

Taking their first tentative steps onto the bridge, the smooth stone hummed to life beneath the party's feet. The flames flickered and grew brighter, as if in greeting.

"Gods, what is this place?" Vick asked.

Cici quivered, breaths picking up fast.

"Gods, everyone…this is an ancient Xitan city!" she squealed.

CHAPTER 8

Scenes depicted among the carvings included all manner of cosmology and ritual. The city's entire history appeared engraved within the oblong tapestry.

"Look," Cici pointed at a few inscribed glyphs. "This is Low Xitan script. There aren't a lot of people who still know how to read it. Can I get a piece of paper?"

"Sure," Andy said, reaching into his backpack. He pulled out a small red journal and chewed-up mechanical pencil. Tearing one page out, he gave it to Cici, who got right to work on her stone-rubbing.

"We could make a fortune with these." Cici said. "Your dad's a historian, right, Vick?"

Vick rolled his eyes. "Man, what are you talking about? You're worried about money right now?"

"Just trying to be shrewd. You gotta take every chance life gives you, right?"

"I'm sure the infinite dark death dungeon is *rife* with opportunity."

"Shut up, Vick," said Drew. "We could use a little optimism right now."

The Vampire made his sigh of disdain *extremely* apparent, pressing further along the bridge. In the meantime, Cici continued her translation, tearing out page after page of Andy's notebook. The boy squirmed; he was *really* hoping to get some more mileage out of the thing.

"Man, this is so cool," Cici squealed with glee. "They've got their whole history here! Look, look! See this one, where they're all like, gathered in a circle?"

"Like they're uh…in a meetin' or somethin'?" Andy asked.

"Yeah! And here, look," Cici pointed to one carving depicting the erection of a grand spire. Drawing from its unique shape, it was easy to decipher which of the many great pillars this carving referred to. Cici tapped Andy on the arm and pointed. Over yonder was the apparent tallest tower, one which just about touched the low bridge.

"That one, right there, that must be important, right?" she asked.

"*Looks* pretty important." Andy said.

"Why don't we go check it out? It doesn't seem too far."

Andy surveyed the sprawling metropolis before them. His heart caught like a lump in his throat.

"I'm not sure." Andy said. "This place is massive. Elena could be anywhere, I mean, she might not even *be here* to begin with."

As if to emphasize Andy's point, a distant, eerie noise loudly clattered. It really could have been anything, be it falling rocks or another chattering beast. Andy's ears twitched in an attempt to pinpoint the source, but the acoustics of this underground city made the task nigh-impossible.

"Maybe these inscriptions could give us a clue?" Cici said. "They might mention some important locations, or…I don't know, some kind of tracking spell?"

Vick scoffed. "Wouldn't that be convenient?"

"I dunno! Maybe they've dealt with kloons before."

"I guess. Do you guys want to try splitting up? We could cover more ground a lot faster that way."

"No," Andy said firmly. "We ought to stick together. The kloons are still down here with us. We can't risk being separated.

I think Cici's right. We should check around and see if there's any information these folks left behind. A map, some old drawings, somethin'. Let's start with that spire."

No further arguments were given. The group approached the low-hanging spire with haste in each step.

A suspended stairway linked the bridge to the tip-top of the inverted tower. The steps defied gravity, individual slabs delicately hanging in midair. Each pale surface looked about as old as it looked frail. Andy's stomach churned.

"Peachy," he muttered.

"I wonder how it works," said Cici. "Like, is it magic? Or magnets?"

"Magic or not, I'm not sure if I trust it." Drew said.

Tanya rolled her eyes and stepped forward, ignoring the others. Seeing her make it relatively okay, the rest nervously followed her lead. A distinct lack of guardrails made every step a deliberate act, each footfall placed with utmost caution.

Drew, second to last, offered Meat-Man a hand while stepping up.

"You good?" Drew asked.

"Long way down." Meat-Man replied.

"Hey, I'm right there with you. C'mon. The ground's more stable up above."

The answer hadn't done much for his anxiety, but it would have to do. The Mycarnid took Drew's hand and tip-toed his way up.

"So Tanya," Vick called as he lazily floated his way up behind her. "What's your take, huh? Think we got a chance at getting out of here?"

The Elf gave a short glance and a thumbs down. Much as she hated to admit it, this whole experience had been rather overwhelming. She knew every inch of the forest up above, but down here? This was all new territory, and it was all a bit much. Still, she couldn't allow herself to falter now. What sort of example would she be setting, displaying fear in the face of a little adversity?

The stairs swayed ever so slightly as they continued their ascent. Each heart pounded with every disjointed crackle of stone.

"Everyone okay?" Drew called.

A chorus of shaky 'yeah's echoed back.

"So these history books of yours," Andy started, walking up behind Cici. "What else have you learned? You know, about the Xita?"

"Oh, lots," Cici said. "Old pantheons, ancient traditions, wars, all kinds of stuff."

"Pantheons?"

Cici beamed. "Yeah, like, do you know the legend of Nanaxiti, for example?"

"Uh, no, never heard of it."

"So basically, Nanaxiti is like, an ancient ancestor to the Xita. Or maybe our *God?* I dunno. She's this giant insect that fell from the stars a bazillion years ago or something and lived deep underground."

"And...she's your *ancestor?*"

"Yeah, kinda. How the legend goes, is like, she ruled over Agartha—center of the Earth—until one day she was 'usurped' by an 'apex predator.' They fought and stuff, and like, it was a *whole thing.*"

'A whole thing' was an understatement. That sounded *insane.* Andy huffed and kept listening.

"After she got killed, it's said Nanaxiti split herself up into a thousand itty-bitty pieces." Cici continued. "And those pieces were what made up the original Xita."

"Hm," Andy tried to picture it in his head. "Pretty cool story."

"It's not just a story—it's the truth! I mean, where else do you think we came from?"

Andy laughed nervously. "I dunno. Giant bugs seem a bit out there. Then again..."

His eyes again graced the city far above.

"...*so's all this.*"

Andy's fists balled tightly, knuckles white with tension. Thankfully, it didn't seem like they had much further to go, as the top, or rather, the bottom of the spire had come within arm's length.

The group at last were met with sanctuary, stepping underneath a stony archway into a wide, circular room. Cici darted toward the center, beaming. The floor's pattern was much like the bridge far below, filled with indecipherable script—tales of ancient happenings. Getting down on her hands and knees, Cici ran her palms across the various bumps. Andy joined her, squinting.

"Can you read any of it?" he asked.

"Not a whole lot, no," Cici said.

There were a few words recognizable from her books—words like 'community,' 'duty,' 'queen'—but one word stuck out, hastily etched near a foreboding glyph.

As she crawled her way over, Cici saw a simple depiction of the inverted city lying above a deep, darkening pit. The stone itself had been artificially dyed, really 'selling' the blackness.

Surely, everyone could easily glean the existence of the outdoor bottomless pit by now. No, what disturbed Cici particularly was what seemed to dwell within the darkness. Embossed linework just barely caught her eye in the low light—a great maw lined with knife-sized incisors. Above the artwork lie one symbol, simply translated, reading:

"*Calamity.*"

Andy couldn't help but feel exposed, the group lying right above this alleged monster like sitting ducks.

"Maybe we should keep going." Andy said. The others nodded, fixed still on the outside..

Their footsteps echoed hollow throughout the building as they climbed out onto the suspended streets above. The quiet metropolis was incredible, if not intimidating.

"This place gives me the creeps," Drew muttered.

"Does it?" Cici asked. "I think it's incredible!"

"Try not to get too attached, we ain't stayin' here for long." Andy said.

"I know. Just trying to drink it all in."

The pace continued, though it was soon cut short. On their search for any signs of life, it seemed they had found it…though not the kind they'd been hoping for.

A cluster of kloons stood motionless in the middle of a long stretch of road. They hadn't noticed the group's presence as of yet, but that could change at any moment. The group got low, pressing themselves against a smooth wall.

"What do we do?" Andy hissed.

Vick chewed nervously on his lower lip. "They don't have your traditional senses, but they can definitely suss out bad vibes."

"'*Bad vibes?*'"

"Strong emotion. It's what they feed on. Fear, anxiety, anger, any of it's fair game. Keep your distance and try not to think about them."

Easier said than done. The city's suspended architecture meant that one wrong move could send them plummeting into the abyss. The narrow walkways did not leave much room to sneak about. Crumbling edges threatened to give way at the slightest disturbance. Andy felt beads of sweat forming at his temples.

Again, Tanya would take the lead. The others followed closely behind, taking each step slower than their lithe companion. Up they climbed, until they devised a 'suitable' detour.

It was the closest one they could reach, anyways.

The walkway they discovered immediately narrowed. They sidestepped along the thin ledge, one after another. It was hardly wide enough to hold their heels. Below, the still-standing kloons looked about as starved as the accompanying abyss.

Meat-Man sidled along, the last to brave the trip. His broad shoulders quivered with every micro-step.

He had nearly crossed the lamentable ledge when a sickening crack echoed throughout the space. The stone beneath his swollen foot gave way, crumbling to dust. The Mycarnid teetered, his new friends' faces frozen. They could only watch as he lost his balance and fell to his doom.

Drew grasped at the empty air where Meat-Man had been standing just moments before—just a bit too late.

The waiting creatures descended upon Meat-Man in a frenzy as soon as his body hit pavement. Their maws widened, revealing rows of jagged teeth. Like piranhas, they tore poor Meat-Man to shreds.

But despite their initial brutality, devouring the Mycarnid did not appear to be on these creatures' agenda. Rather than enjoy their fine dining, they began to assemble like ants, carrying the Mycarnid's individual limbs in groups toward the heart of the city. Their mercy was almost coordinated.

Miraculously, Meat-Man was still alive, though he'd been reduced to modular chunks of his former glory. His stolen head looked concerned to say the least, disappearing into the dark with the bouncing bodies.

Andy knew venturing into the kloons' domain was tantamount to suicide. The thought of abandoning someone to such a grim fate, however, was equally unbearable.

"We *have* to go after him." Andy said.

Tanya nodded—she was already scoping out the path of least resistance.

Vick and Drew exchanged uncertain glances, the Vampire floating back a bit, arms crossed.

Andy huffed. "You ain't gonna just let him die, are you?"

Drew rubbed the back of his neck. "It's not that I *want* to, but we have to think about this. You saw what just happened. Imagine what those things would do to one of us."

"Well, yeah, but…I mean, if we don't try, what does that make us?"

"Hey, in case you forgot, he tried to *eat us* earlier." Vick said.

"I know, but he was probably just *scared*. I mean, *Drew's* sure he ain't a bad guy. Why can't *you* be?"

Vick rolled his eyes. "That isn't the gotcha you think it is."

Drew nearly spoke, venom building in his tongue. He would not act on this impulse, however. Andy already had it covered.

"Alright, Mr. Cynical." Andy said. "If you don't trust *him*, then trust *me.*"

"What, after everything you pulled last summer?"

Cici frowned. "Vick…"

"No, shut up. I'm right. *Why* should we trust you? Don't forget, *buddy*, you straight up *lied* to us last time we trusted you. Sold us out for your freaking 'cure.' How'd that work out, huh? Where'd that get us? Because it seems like everything started going downhill the moment you showed up. You may have tricked everyone else here into thinking you make good calls, but *not* me. Gods, even if we weren't *trapped* down here, we'd be screwed anyway, just wondering when The Order's gonna come and wipe us off the map."

"Well we *are* stuck down here." Andy said.

"Right, and I'm stuck with *you*. You stupid hick, you don't know the first thing about this place, why should I listen to—?"

"*Vick*," Drew loudly whispered. The Vampire huffed and looked about, noting that all his companions were locked staring into the darkness. He heard the scuttling of tiny claws across the floor, one stray kloon stepping out into the light. Its fat nose twitched.

The party held their breath. The kloon turned and waddled away, back toward its 'friends.'

Everyone let out a slow breath. Drew slowly turned to Andy, scarred eye twitching. "Full disclosure, I don't like this, either, kid. Your safety is *my* responsibility. You really expect us to go diving headfirst into *that*?"

"I think we owe it to him." Andy said. "*I* do, anyway."

Drew held Andy's gaze for a long moment, then let out an exasperated breath. Meat-Man was *his* friend, too. The kid was right. Unfortunately.

"We scope the place out, save any skin that's convenient." Drew said. "But that's it. We're not sticking our necks out for the *whole freakin' city*—the *Rangers* can handle that."

Funny he should mention that; they hadn't seen head nor hide of the Rangers since they'd fallen down. Andy imagined there must be a lot of ground for the troops to cover, both above and below. He just hoped that it wouldn't be too late by the time they found the missing others.

The decision made for them, everyone cautiously descended from the ledge, following the path the kloons had taken with their fungal friend. Andy passed by a stationary Vick without a word, his gaze fixed to the floor. Silence was only broken by the scuffling of feet and the crackling of eternal torches.

Smooth elegance in the architecture gave way to jagged, twisted structures as they approached the upper levels of the city. Like the buildings were being warped by an unseen force.

Somehow, it felt *alive.*

Tanya held up a hand and pointed ahead—a square of tall buildings, all surrounding a faint glow. The scattered limbs of their Mycarnid friend were left haphazardly strewn about on one path leading toward the center.

Andy could feel his heart sink into his stomach. Something pulsated up ahead.

"I'll take point," Drew said, stepping forward. "Stay close and keep quiet."

They crept forward, hugging the walls of the alley, approaching the sound of a dull hum.

Drew gagged as he bore witness to the glow's source. Sandwiched between the towers and hanging from the distant ceiling was a gigantic, pulsating mass of sickly yellowed flesh.

The mass was easily the size of a city block, hung like a grotesque chandelier, surface glistening with the sheen of mucus. Ropey tendrils extended from the central mass, anchoring it to the stone above and the buildings which surrounded it, buildings partially absorbed by the putrid pustule.

A low, rhythmic thrumming pulsed from within, rattling the party's teeth, making their eardrums sore. Bulky sacs dotted the hive's surface, some breathing gently, others twitching, spasming, as though something inside was trying to fight its way out.

Drew covered his mouth with one hand, the rotten smell threatening to relieve him of his lunch.

"That's a hive if I've ever seen one." Cici said. She looked more impressed than horrified.

Andy let a quick breath out. "Okay. How do we want to do this?"

"We set it on fire." Vick said.

"Not yet, you're not. Meat-Man's in there."

"Whatever we do, we need to be fast." Drew said. "Vick, you keep watch. Turn invisible, float up in there, I don't care, just make sure you have an eye on us. Andy, you try to find people in there. Use your nose. Our main target's Meat-Man, anyone else comes second. We should double up and work in pairs. Too many of us in one spot might draw attention."

"I'll go with Andy." Cici said.

"Then Tanya, you're with me," said Drew. "Does everybody understand what we're doing?"

They all nodded collectively. Vick, muttering a spell to himself, was instantly cloaked in magic mist, his form vanishing. The others went on ahead, trying not to think too hard about what exactly they were climbing into.

The air was heavy enough with the stench of rot. It needn't be heavier with their moods.

Several shapes scuttled across the hive's surface—kloons by the dozens, crawling in and out, honking loudly all the while. Thankfully, they paid the approaching party no mind...*for now.*

There were several openings, like large honeycombs, dotting the hive's surface. Andy and Cici moved for the one closest to the ground, where kloons traffic appeared low. Drew and Tanya made a more vertical entrance.

Slipping through an oozing orifice, Andy and Cici navigated the hive's inner walls with the utmost caution. The fleshy corridor stretched out, gooey walls undulating with every 'heartbeat.' Viscous fluid seeped from the ceiling and pooled onto the soft floor. *Like walking through a blister-covered bouncy castle,* Cici thought.

The two friends shared a gag. *How abominable.* The first space they came across was filled with those same bulbous sacs as the surface. Each sac twitched with life—not that of the kloons, but humanoids, people—the very citizens Andy watched be taken from the surface.

It was not sheer horror that captivated the teens' eyes, however. No, amidst all the chaos, unmistakable to the two, was the presence of several armored figures, waltzing freely about. Knights of the Natural Order, polished armor dribbling with the surrounding condensation. They hadn't been jailed by the kloons, in fact, they all moved in tandem with one another, marching with a shared purpose. Associates. Coworkers. Partners in crime.

One group of knights congregated around a pitiful form, one left behind by their rat-like allies. It was all that remained of Meat-Man.

His severed head looked back and forth, terror in his bloodshot eyes. One towering figure, sporting a grotesque set of armor, reached down and grabbed Meat-Man by his tattered cap.

"Well, lookie what we have here. Never seen one of you, before. What brings you to our humble abode?"

CHAPTER 9

Meat-Man's jaw twitched. His fear—as well as his lack of vocal cords—rendered him mute. The large man's sneer grew wider.

"No matter," he said as he lowered the creature's head. "You'll serve your purpose soon enough."

"Say, you wanna play a round of footie with it?" another knight piped up.

"I'd rather not get the little bastards riled up. We're on a tight schedule. Set it in with the others."

The second knight slouched as he took Meat-Man's head. "Aye, sir."

Andy and Cici ducked back behind cover.

"We can *not* leave him with these guys." Cici said.

"Ain't sure there's much we can do, until they all leave."

Cici frowned, but nodded. "Okay, maybe we can come back around for him. Can you smell the others? Elena?"

Andy's nose twitched. *Sniff, sniff. Eugh.*

"…Can't make out much of anythin' here."

"Okay. No pressure." Cici said. She only half-meant it.

What to do? There were multiple guards stationed throughout the hive—not a terribly large amount, but enough to prove a substantial threat should they raise the alarm.

"Maybe I could distract them?" Cici asked.

The idea was considered, chewed on for a moment. Andy didn't want to put his friend in any more danger than he already had. Plus, again, that ran the risk of raising the alarm.

Circling back to his observations, one bit *did* stick out to Andy, that being the narrow side passage that seemed to go *behind* the pustules. Like a service door for the nasty little things.

"How 'bout there? I betcha this leads to another part of the hive—maybe."

Cici shrugged. She didn't see another way forward, and it wasn't like tight spaces particularly bothered her.

"Sure, yeah, that sounds good to me."

"Not me," said Vick. The Vampire uncloaked himself, arms crossed. He tapped his foot impatiently.

"You're not keeping an eye on the others?" Cici asked.

"They can handle themselves. I'm more worried about you two doing something stupid."

"Oh yeah?" Andy growled. "*Everything* I do is stupid, right? I might as well commit."

"That isn't—I'm just—I can't follow you in there. I can't. If you go any farther, you're gonna be on your own for a bit. I'll uh...stay back and try to help Monster-Man."

Rather exhausted with Vick for the day, Andy was not opposed. He could excuse the Vampire for being a claustrophobe if it meant some peace and quiet. Andy turned back toward the tight tunnel.

For the first time in a while, there wasn't a hint of sarcasm in Vick's voice.

"Just be careful. *Please.*"

It caught Andy off guard, but he gave an earnest nod back. "We will. Pinky promise."

Vick rolled his eyes and held up a pinky. "Sure."

The two locked fingers.

Just then, a guard began to shout.

"Hey, I think I see something—hey!"

"*Shucks,*" Andy released Vick from his grip. "I'll see you soon."

Vick nodded. "See you."

Guards approaching, Andy and Cici squeezed into the passage, while Vick vanished once again.

Andy could see why the Vampire was so hesitant to enter this space. The tunnel was steamy, humid, quite difficult to breathe in. It didn't help that the membranous walls were pushing in on them from all sides. They were forced to shuffle from side-to-side, pressing their hands against the slimy flesh that encased them.

Cici cringed as she moved past one lump, clearly holding a whole person inside. A face pressed up against the membrane, contorted in terror. It weakly mouthed a plea for help. The Xita pressed her hand against the cocoon.

"W-we're gonna get help soon, just hang tight."

More and more of the occupants' forms came into focus. Most of their faces were obscured by milky membrane, but a scarce few could be identified—especially when the 'breathing' of the hive forcibly squashed Andy's face against the lumps.

Some folks he knew from a distance, like the local radio host, Mr. Squawker, or the Minotaur that owned the restaurant on main street. Some faces, like Geb's, hit much closer to home.

The kloons really got most everyone.

The tunnel did, in fact, lead to another room eventually, one which appeared to be lacking in guards. Lucky. Though perhaps they were merely taking a bathroom break.

Still, it stirred an innate interest—who were they keeping in here, particularly? Who was considered 'low-priority' by The Order?

Just as soon as he realized it, Andy froze.

These weren't Supernaturals being kept in here; these were Humans.

Among the many faces held within the pods, one stuck out to Andy like a sore thumb—that of his father, Martin. His bearded mug was out cold, smushed up against the wall of a particularly swollen cocoon.

Andy ran to his father's prison, Cici following not far behind. He did his best to try and rip open the sac with his claws.

"Mr. Kessler?" Cici asked. "This doesn't make any sense. I thought The Order's whole deal was like...to *protect* Humans? Why would they—?"

"I don't know. I don't want to know. Help me."

"R-right."

With their combined effort, the two friends managed to tear a hole through the pustule, and in a flood of sugar water, Martin spilled out onto the ground. He immediately sputtered, fountains of slimy fluid spewing from his mouth. Andy helped turn him onto his side.

"Dad, c'mon," he said, trying to keep his voice low.

Martin's eyes fluttered open, unfocused and glazed over. He coughed a few more times.

"Andy?" he asked.

"We gotta go, now."

Martin struggled to sit up. "What's going on?"

Andy grabbed his arm and helped Martin to his feet.

"Short version—I think these knights kidnapped everyone. We're in some kind of hive-thing underground. We're trying to find Elena and get outta here."

"It's true, Mr. Kessler," Cici said with a vigorous nod.

A cough echoed from the hallway, followed by the clanking of metal boots. Andy's body tensed.

"Someone's coming." he said.

The group made their way back toward the thin crack in the wall, Martin leaning on Andy for support. However, when they passed by another cluster of cocoons, Andy froze up. Through the membrane, he could make out Elena's sleeping face, floating blissfully, peacefully, unaware.

Andy looked from her to the exit. The clanking grew louder, a maggot-shaped shadow creeping along the wall. The grotesque knight was almost upon them.

"Andy, we have to go," Cici said, antennae pinned back against her head.

Grunting, Andy pushed his father towards her. "Get him out of here," he ordered, turning back to Elena's cocoon.

His claws tore into the fleshy sac. The membrane split, spilling Elena and a torrent of liquid onto the floor. Andy scooped the girl up in his arms, her small body limp and cold.

The looming shadow was mere seconds away from rounding the corner. In a haste, Andy leapt toward the exit, Elena clutched tightly to his chest. He was careful not to suffocate her, allowing her chin to rest on his shoulder as he squeezed his way through.

The coughing man entered. His lips sneered beneath his helmet, head scanning from left to right. Andy could hear his pace picking up. They only had a bit of time before the whole hive was on their tails.

He could only hope Drew and Tanya had done their part.

Shuffling through slimy walls—they grew tighter with every second. Cici constantly checked behind herself as she led the charge.

A shrill alarm pierced the veil, the fleshy corridor undulating with the sound. Andy grit his teeth, unable to cover his ears. He had to power through.

Emerging into the main chamber, chaos had erupted. Knights were scrambling in all directions, kloons oozed from every crevice, all of them converging fast on the escapees.

The party darted toward the exit, the outside seeming so close, yet just out of reach. It was like a nightmare, the soft ground swallowing their feet with every step, further slowing their pace.

A few odd kloons hopped on their backs, gnawing their flesh, giggling all the while. Martin was still weak from his time in the cocoon, but Cici hauled him along with a surprising amount of gusto. She pulled, determined not to let go, and they managed to reach the cold stone streets of the Xitan metropolis.

The boy wasn't far behind. Just as Andy's soles touched stable ground, it was like a second wind. He narrowly dashed out of the way of a swinging knight, feeling the back of his shirt clipped by the tip of the blade.

Just above, Tanya and Drew hopped onto an upper walkway. With her own magic pact, Tanya could create a simple wall of thorns behind to block a number of her chasers. Not nearly enough, though. There were far too many openings, and zero time to shut them down.

For now they ran as fast as they could. Dangling from Drew's hip, Meat-Man's head appeared 'rescued' as well, though apparently displeased.

A flash of otherworldly light lit up from within the hive. The ensuing screech chilled the party's bones. Multiple sacs split open, and from within, malformed, mountainous blobs of fuzz fell out.

Kloonpiles—relatives of the kloon—overgrown variants of the skittering pests. Their disturbingly wide grins stretched all the way around their heads, and their eyes were beginning to look like horns. Writhing inside of their swollen bodies were various growths bearing faces of their own—more kloons to soon be birthed.

They were as disgusting as they were dangerous, and a good number of them were closing in on the gang's position when the knights couldn't.

Vick bought them some additional time—a glorious fireball blasted the ground behind the crew, forcing the knights to stop altogether. It was unlucky, then, that the fire didn't seem to stop the raging charge of the kloonpiles—all it really seemed to do was make them angrier.

Andy wiped his eyes. His lungs burned. Elena's limp form bounced against his chest. The streets blurred past, a maze of lovely stones. Cici's voice was all that cut through to him.

"Up there! Look!"

She pointed giddily, upward at the cavern ceiling. Andy followed, squinting through the dim. High above, hardly visible amidst the moss, a metallic glint caught their eye. A grate of sorts, part of the city's old aqueduct system. *Bingo.*

"Everyone, start heading up!" Andy said.

The lower duo veered sharply, making for a set of stairs zigzagging up the cavern walls. Drew held back a moment to take Cici's place as Martin's chauffeur.

"Long time, no see, old man." Drew said.

"Not long enough." Martin replied.

They were almost there. The sewer grate loomed close, a rusty beacon of hope within arms reach. Water still trickled through these ancient pipes, a soothing melody in contrast to the approaching violence.

Drew and Tanya worked together to pry the grate open. They didn't dare look behind. Kloonpiles were already scaling the walls with alarming speed, their amorphous bodies jiggling, their massive talons finding purchase of the old stone.

The duo strained against rusted metal, muscles bulging with effort. The grate creaked and groaned, centuries of corrosion fighting their every move. Flakes of rust sprinkled down.

"Come on, you bastard," Drew growled. He braced his foot against the wall.

Tanya's bark-like scars looked as though they were going to peel from how taut her skin was being pulled. She yanked with all her might. With one last ear-splitting shriek, the grate gave way. It swung open on hinges that hadn't moved in eons, the damp dark of sanctuary lying ahead.

"Go, go!" Andy shouted. Martin and Drew climbed in first, followed by Tanya, then Cici.

Behind them, the first of many kloonpiles reached the top of the wall. It continued to hurdle its way toward the group at break-neck speed. Dozens of faces writhed within its bulk, each grinning just as maniacally as the last.

With the help of everyone up top, Andy was pulled into the safe space. They huddled, away from the opening, and Tanya fought to close the grate. The kloonpiles pressed in, slamming their heads into the metal over and over again. Drew went to help the Elf, and with a final herculean effort, the two managed to get the grate shut. An ancient locking mechanism engaged with a resounding clang.

All was still, all beyond the banging outside. Andy sagged against the wet wall, his legs giving out on him.

"Safe," he sighed, allowing his eyes to rest. His chest heaved up and down, over and over. The adrenaline ebbed from his system. Things were going to be okay.

As the initial panic had subsided, the group had settled in for a moment of zen. They could feel the tension in their muscles unwind, replaced now by exhaustion which cut to the bone.

Andy cradled Elena's head all the while. Her eyelids flitted, a groan rattling in her throat. The others gathered around.

"Elena? Can you hear me?" Andy asked. He brushed a strand of damp hair from her forehead.

The girl's eyes opened, unfocused at first. She tried to sit up immediately, to assess the unfamiliar surroundings, but Andy gently held her in place.

"It's okay. You're safe now."

"Where are we?" Elena asked.

"It's a long story."

"We're in a Xitan aqueduct!" Cici said.

"Best not to overwhelm her with too much right now," said Martin.

Andy nodded. "We're underground, and we don't wanna be." The boy looked around, pressing his lips together. "Now where we go from here's the question."

"That *is* the question, isn't it," Vick said, fiddling with his earring. "Cici, you're the expert. What do you say?"

"Well, so obviously, the aqueducts are leading water in from... *somewhere*. My guess is there's a well up above—maybe we're under the lake—if we get up nearer to the surface, I bet there's some alternate path we could take to get back home."

"We might have to swim our way out. How long can you guys hold your breaths?" Drew asked.

"Definitely not long enough," Andy said, feeling himself choke up at the thought of it. "Guess we'll find out soon enough though, huh?"

Cici pointed a finger downward, tracing it in the opposite direction of the water's flow. "This way ought to work for now."

Andy looked at Elena.

"You think you'll be able to walk for a bit, bud?" he asked.

"I think so." Elena said, sniffling.

"Alright. Dad?"

Martin nodded. "I'll be fine."

With all said and done, the group followed Cici's directions and trudged on through the old tunnel. Elena stuck close to Tanya. The Ranger was one of her only fleeting comforts in this kloon-infested hellscape.

Vick provided some much-needed light, a small orb of flickering flame hovering above his outstretched palm. His shoulders hunched, his usual swagger replaced with weariness.

Sensing an opportunity here, Andy looked up to his father. His expression indicated a sort of pleading; Martin understood, giving Andy a small nudge.

"Go ahead."

Giving a thankful smile, Andy quickened his pace to catch up with Vick.

"Hey," Andy said, falling in step beside him.

"Hey." Vick replied. Andy cleared his throat.

"You uh…doing okay?"

"What? Yeah. I'm fine."

Another beat of silence passed. Vick spoke again, voice subdued. "Look, about earlier—"

"It's fine. You were right. I totally screwed you guys."

"I wasn't going to say that," Vick sighed. "I was a jerk. I shouldn't have called you stupid."

"Are you apologizing?"

"Yes, as a matter of fact."

"Well, it's...*okay*. I mean, it's *not* okay, but, I get it. We're all on edge. This whole situation's—"

"Wretched?"

"Yeah. Wretched works."

Vick sighed. "Anyways. I know I'm a *massive* tool under pressure. I just want you guys to know I'm uh...I'm grateful you came to save me."

"Aw, shucks. You know we couldn't make it out of here without you. I'm always happy to have you on my team. Really."

The Vampire cleared his throat, uncomfortable with the sincerity of the moment. He had to squeeze in a quip of some kind.

"*Somebody's* gotta keep you mere mortals out of trouble."

Andy scoffed. "Like you're not the one always stirrin' the pot."

"I'm working on it."

Andy looked down at his feet, kicking a pebble that found itself in his path.

"You think this'll make for a good story?" Andy asked.

"Oh, no question." Vick said. "This is gonna be the talk of the town for-freaking-ever."

"Hey, there you go. Look at you being optimistic."

"*Tch*. I'm not some hopeless cynic, you know."

"What would *you* call it then?"

"I prefer the term 'realist.'" Vick lifted his chin haughtily.

"I think you're a geek."

The two came to a pause, passing an old carving on the wall. Hypnotic, spiraling patterns shimmered faintly in Vick's magical light.

"Woah. Look at that," Andy said, running his fingers over the carvings.

Vick leaned in closer, brow furrowed.

"Huh, yeah. That's actually kind of beautiful," he paused. "As beautiful as a sewer gets, anyways."

"Of course. Wouldn't want anyone thinking you actually appreciate anything neat, right?"

"Hey guys," Cici called. "Can we get a light? Something's blocked the way."

Vick cleared his throat. "Right, yeah. Be over in a sec."

The blockage came into view as the Vampire approached. It looked to be some kind of cave in, though it was unlike any he'd seen, all fuzzy and covered in...*moss?*

Cici recoiled first, realizing what it was. What she had initially mistaken for rubble was, in fact, a calcified cluster of kloons. Their once-vibrant fur was now matted and overgrown with a slimy green coat. Their weathered-down faces were unreadable.

Mesmerizing, revolting, perhaps a mixture of the two; it was a sculpture of nightmares. The blockage stretched from the floor to the ceiling, completely sealing off the tunnel ahead.

Andy's nose wrinkled at the horrid odor.

"They must've been stuck down here for a long time." Cici said.

A faint movement caught Vick's eye. He leaned in closer, when suddenly, a small section of the mass began to twitch and writhe. Mossy limbs struggled against their calcified brethren, fighting to break free. Muffled squeaks and giggles echoed throughout the cavern.

Somebody just woke up.

The group began to back away, until Martin snapped them out of stunned silence with an order.

"Run, fool!"

Just as they did, entire sections of the blockage wrenched themselves free. Collective fear acted like a clarion call, rousing the ancient beings from their slumber.

A cluster, no larger than a basketball, broke away from the larger mass first. They tumbled, shaking off centuries of moss and grime. One locked its faded, false eyes on Andy. Its grin stretched wide, revealing rows of jagged needles.

Right back the way they came. The party fled, splashing through shallow water, the sound of tiny claws scrabbling the stone behind them.

There was the grate they came through—but they couldn't go back that way, not with the miniature army surely in waiting.

"Keep going," Martin barked. "There's got to be another way out!"

The honking chorus grew louder, punctuated by the sound of more bodies breaking free from stone. Andy dared a glance over his shoulder, immediately regretting it. The writhing mass of mosses quickly gained.

Vick's flames bobbed precariously above his fingertips, casting long shadows on the blurred walls. The light revealed a glint up ahead—another grate.

"*There*," Andy said, sliding to a stop. "Help me get it open!"

Both him and Drew gripped the rusted bars, straining with all their might. Tanya joined, adding her strength to theirs. The grate groaned in protest.

"*Hurry,*" Cici shrieked, watching the approaching horde.

Vick raised the fire above his head.

"*Incende!*"

Reacting to his words, the fireball bloated into a blitz of hot air. Vick lobbed it toward the crowd, a good number of kloons set ablaze in the ensuing explosion.

In a cosmically bad streak of luck, one of the kloons, now a flaming torpedo, was sent right into Vick's face from the blast. The Vampire was knocked into a blind daze. Cici caught him before he hit his head on the stone.

Martin stepped up to the grate in the meantime, placing his hands next to the youths'.

"On three," he commanded. "One…two…*three!*"

The four of pulled with everything they had, their combined strength overcoming the mechanism at last. With a screech, the grate swung wide open.

Andy and Drew hopped down to the waiting bridge, both of them assisting Elena before allowing the others to follow.

Cici walked Vick toward the grate—but before she could reach the opening, a number of the mossy creatures latched onto her ankles, holding her down. The dampness of the aqueduct had already extinguished Vick's righteous flames, and following it, the fuzzy flood had come to overwhelm the both of them.

Letting out a cry, Cici shoved Vick with all her might—he stumbled, tripping, spilling out of the grate and landing flat on his face.

"Cici, come on," Andy said, reaching for her hand.

The Xita screamed, fighting with all her might to lift her legs. The river of kloons had become far too much, however, its powerful currents threatening to pull her under.

There was only so much time to absorb the fear in her eye. In a flash of fluff, Cici was utterly consumed.

CHAPTER 10

Andy's heart fluttered.

"*No!*" he wailed. Before he could venture into the river of beasts to rescue her, his father's arms encircled him. Martin pulled back with all the might he could muster.

"Son, we gotta move, now!" Martin said. Forcefully, he turned Andy right around and shoved him along down the path.

The rest of the group had already retreated, jostling each other as they looked for any hint of sanctuary. An already unfamiliar landscape had since twisted into a labyrinthian horror. They pushed forward, downward, toward the respite of the spanning bridge far below. A relentless swarm nipped at their heels, close enough to taste their terror.

"Dead end!" Drew shouted up ahead.

The words hit like a punch to the gut. Andy tried to anchor himself, to proceed as rationally as he could, but the rationality of his mind was quickly reduced each time he saw those wretched things hot on their trail.

"Over here!" Vick said. His voice cut above the tumult, a thin thread of hope. The group veered sharply.

Andy's gaze locked on to a stone door ahead—Tanya was already there, grabbing the chain mechanism tight and pulling with fearful force.

With a desperate lurch, everyone squeezed themselves beneath the heavy door one by one.

Tanya heaved, arms strained against the relentless pull of gravity. She bought the group time, sure, seconds that stretched into lifelines—but Tanya could already feel the pull of the tide, a stream of malignant glee rapidly piling at her ankles.

Andy was through the door first. Vick ran in second, assisted by Drew—his eyes were bloodshot, full of tears, a burn across his face. Martin and Elena followed last, the little girl choked up on fearful sobs.

The kloons were already flooding in—a few seconds more, and they would be overwhelmed, drowned in the things. Though Drew had turned to grab the chain on the other side, Tanya was already up to her waist in the creatures. She felt herself being dragged away.

In that last moment, the Elf's eyes met with Andy's. A silent conversation happened between the two.

Her hand let go of the chain.

The door slammed shut, crushing the remaining scuttling kloons beneath it. A series of violent stomps later, and the rest that had made it in were dispatched as well. What little atmosphere they had was smothering, the scent of damp sticking to the backs of their throats almost as much as the sugar. The interior was unsurprisingly dark, suffocating and musty, a forgotten relic that could as well be a prison as it was salvation. Its walls felt as though they were closing in with that wave of terror not far behind. A shrill chorus of claws continued to scrape up against the old stone until eventually petering out.

Andy struggled to process everything he'd witnessed. The world was blurry, distorted, reality warping under the weight of his grief. The boy slowly faced the others, mechanical, rigid.

Vick's lips moved fast, but Andy couldn't hear a thing. It was as if someone had hit the mute button on everything. The only sound penetrating the fog was a high-pitched ringing.

In Drew's corner was nothing but a husk. In contrast to Vick pacing, he sat eerily still since they settled down. His skin was almost deflated, he cowered as though he hoped to be invisible. Guilt was etched into every line of his face, aging him years in mere seconds.

As for Martin and Elena, the both of them huddled together near a chunky column. Martin's face was a case study in conflicting emotion. Elena, shockingly enough, clung to him tight. She had expected the horrors to materialize from stone itself. In this instance, her hatred for the man could briefly subside in favor of solace.

Shock would recede, now replaced with a tide of rage. Andy's hands clenched at his sides, claws digging into his skin.

First his mom, now his friends—why did bad things always seem to happen to him? What did *he* do to deserve *this*?

Without warning, Andy's fist connected with the nearest wall. The impact shot a hollow pain through his arm, but it hardly registered. Again, and again, he pounded the stone, each blow accompanied by a guttural scream. The echoes of his voice reverberating in his ears only further added to his overstimulation.

Vick's monologue stopped abruptly. He watched, biting his lower lip, wincing with every punch.

Andy's knuckles split open, leaving behind smears of crimson on the stone. The pain was nothing but a dull throb compared to it all.

Screaming gave way to hefty, heaving sobs. Andy's tears mingled with the blood on his hands as they fell. The fight drained from his body.

Martin put a hand on Andy's shoulder.

"Hey, boy." he said. The man did his best to mask his gruff voice.

Andy's tear-streaked face further crumpled. He collapsed into his old man, burying his face in Martin's shoulder. He was like a fortress, built to weather the storm tearing his son apart.

"I've got you, boy," Martin said, continuing to rub Andy's back. "I've got you."

Elena clung to them as well, as though afraid the two may disappear. The world around them faded away, the warmth of embrace accompanying the steady beat of their hearts.

A small island of comfort, amidst a sea of loss.

It wasn't clear to Vick how he could possibly comfort any of them right now. With a stiff hand, he reached out to touch Andy's back. He waited for guidance, but knew it wouldn't come.

Drew's brooding only further intensified. It was like an invisible thunderstorm brewed over his head. His fingers twitched, rubbing against each other in perpetual, agitated motion. His face was dark, teeth grinding together. His lips moved silently, forming words only he could hear. Plans, promises, oaths of revenge, retribution—they all danced on the edge of his tongue. Ready for a fight that had yet to happen.

Pulling back slightly, Andy's red-rimmed eyes met his father's. Though words often failed them both, there was a quiet understanding that the two shared. Through thick and thin, they would get through it together...or at least, that's what Andy had hoped.

With their adventure's most recent turn, that hope had begun to waste away.

The group was frozen in their tableau of grief, for a few minutes longer at least. But as time continued to march on, they came to the realization that they'd have to leave this place at one point or another. Whatever waited for them on the other side wouldn't be pretty.

"So...what now?" Vick asked. Drew's looked at Meat-Man, still tied to one of his belt loops. Sighing, he untied the live cranium and pressed his forehead against it.

"I think, right now, we need to focus more on survival than anything else. We're clearly not getting out of the underground any time soon."

"No, don't say that. There needs to be another way, there's—"

"There's nothing, Vick. There's nothing for us down here, nothing but death, and…and *sugar*," the man slumped over again. "We're not getting out on our own, face it. Might as well lock ourselves up somewhere safe while we wait for the Rangers to show up. *If* they show up."

"*Okay*…so what do you have in mind? Like, say we hunker down, I don't think here's the place for it."

"I'd say all we have to go off of is Meat-Man's place. Wherever that may be. Maybe we lay low there for a while," Drew looked at his friend's still-breathing head. "Is that alright with you, big man?"

Meat-Man gave a few quiet blinks in response.

"What about food?" Vick asked. "Water?"

"I don't know. We'll figure it out."

"We better start with finding another way out of this building," Martin said, pressing his ear against the door. "I can still hear 'em scuttlin' around out there."

Vick nodded, muttering beneath his breath. Once more, a tiny ball of fire burst from his palm, floating in place and bringing light to the blackened room.

The group saw themselves occupying a blocky chamber, its purpose long since obscured by the ravages of time. The flickering firelight danced across the cracked walls and desks. One desk, marred in gouges and dust, sat square in the left-hand corner of the room. Behind it, rows of cubbies held rolls of parchment. The setup resembled a post office of sorts.

Drew approached the desk, running his fingers along its surface, brushing away the centuries of grime to reveal an ornate insignia carved into the wood, like an eye surrounded on all sides by spikes. Curious, Elena pulled a scroll from its respective cubby. Looking over the strange symbols, however, she was unable to glean anything significant.

Martin spotted a doorway partially obscured by one of the stone columns.

"Over here," he called, gesturing for the others to follow.

The doorway led to a set of stairs, rather uneven. At the bottom of the stairs, another massive door blocked their path, secured by another mechanism. Drew went to go and give the chain a pull, though he was stopped by a shaking Andy.

"Careful. We can't make too much noise."

"Yeah, yeah." Drew said. The man gave a few test pulls to gauge the strength he'd need, then, with questionable precision, he pulled the chain downward. The door rose, every skid of stone against stone startling the others. Their poor hearts couldn't take the anticipation.

Once it was raised a good amount, Martin passed under the door and grabbed a hold of the chain on the other side. After everyone passed through, the old man slowly and carefully allowed the slab to lower to the floor.

They stood on yet another ledge, overlooking the massive bridge they came in on. It looked so small from their vantage point, like a splinter of stone. The distance seemed daunting.

"That's our way out." Andy said. Martin swallowed back some nervous bile. He'd been brought down here while unconscious, yet to see the sheer scale of the impossible city.

Drew peered over the edge, pointing to a series of outcroppings stuck out precariously from the nearest building. There was a vague path he could imagine, one that led them right back toward the main spire.

"We might be able to climb down there." he said.

It was a treacherous descent, every step feeling like a risk. Stone would occasionally squawk. The gaping maw below felt wider every time they looked down.

Every minute felt like an hour. The bridge below grew steadily larger, no longer a mere thread.

Skittering from above sent a jolt of panic through everyone. Their heads snapped up, eyes collectively bulging as they caught glimpses of something fuzzy moving their way. Stealth no longer a concern, the group climbed as fast as their arms would carry them toward the spire.

Elena rode piggyback on Martin the whole time, hanging on for dear life. The old man was unsure if he'd be able to keep it up at this rate.

But at last, they reached the upper base of the tower. Fear swapped places with hope, with the grand mural coming into view. Almost there—they were almost free from the hive.

One by one, the party stepped down the suspended staircase. Each of them struggled with looking down to ensure their proper footing. Every glance spared was a reminder of that horrible, hungry abyss.

Finally, though, solid ground—the group reached the bridge with a collective sigh of relief. The structure stretched on toward the mouth of the distant cave, one last stretch. They hurriedly scampered across.

Andy led the charge. Vick followed close, guided by his hand.

Elena, still riding piggyback, buried her face into Martin's skull. She didn't want to gaze at the dizzying drop. Martin was just glad this marathon was almost over.

Drew brought up the rear, clutching Meat-Man's head with one hand, keeping it steady against his thigh. If he made it out of this alive, there was surely a song to come out of it.

The promise of shelter, their hope swelling—as they reached the threshold, their hearts sank like rocks. Marching feet echoed, growing louder. Everyone skidded to a halt.

End of the line.

From the darkness emerged a row of knights. They moved militantly, forming an impenetrable wall across the cave's mouth. From behind the wall of shields, the ringleader made his grand appearance.

Coughing, laughing, coming to a stop before the group, his helm was like the face of a hungry botfly.

"Going so soon?" the stranger rasped.

Drew saw red, picking up into a running pace. Several crossbows were pointed his way. He stopped, though his eyes never strayed from the maggot's gaze.

Martin recognized those gnarly teeth anywhere—his prior assailant's, Angstrom Brown's. The old man let Elena down onto the ground.

"I figured your greasy hide had something to do with this."

"Who's he?" Andy asked.

"Angstrom Brown," Martin sneered. "Another lapdog of The Natural Order."

"Please, Kessler. Brown's my *civilian* name. When I'm at work, you will call me 'milord.'"

Vick scoffed. "Yeah, right. You're the lord of jack."

Brown tut-tutted, pacing toward the group. "Oh, contraire. I am a lord of stains, a liege to grime, a scion of sludge. My purpose is to bring as much *filth* and *depravity* as I can to you *loathsome* creatures. I am a lord most vulgar—among my ranks, I am called Vulgo."

"I don't give a damn who you are," Drew growled. "What did you do with Cici?"

"Your friends are all safe with me, for now. You all had better cooperate if you would like them to stay that way."

"And the Humans?" Andy asked. "What sense is there in lockin' them up? Here I thought you was on the same side."

Vulgo shrugged. "A focus group, nothing more. A means to an end."

"What end is that, I wonder?" Martin asked. "Food for your pests?"

"On the contrary, I need you all very much alive. You see, you all make up the fundamental building blocks for my ongoing efforts at 'rejuvenation.'"

"Uhuh? What are you gettin' at?"

"I'm sure you've realized it by now, but we are not *alone* on this planet. No, we have to share it with these…" Vulgo gestured.

"…*mutants*. Creations of a short-sighted God, one bored of his playthings. They have power far beyond what you and I are capable of. *We* are the rightful heirs to this planet, make no mistake…but we are weak, Kessler; weak in the face of our contemporaries. I am going to make us *strong* again."

Martin squirmed. "How so?"

"Through science, study, and, of course, with this," Vulgo produced a bronze amulet with a glowing amethyst at its center— Martin recognized it immediately as the heirloom he'd hidden away.

Vulgo laughed. "What's the matter? You look like you've seen a ghost."

"Brown," Martin raised a tempering hand. "You need to listen—"

The loathsome lord thrust the heirloom forward. A blast of energy shot from the amethyst. It struck Martin in the chest, blowing him back several feet. The man slid to a stop, coughing his lungs out. He'd nearly fallen from the bridge by the time the others got to him.

Cosmic magic, the absolute scent of it; it immediately caught Vick's attention. He knew this power. The Vampire shot a look at Vulgo. Smoke rose from the knight's assaulting arm. *Curious.*

"I've seen one of those before," Vick said. "A Carcosan Heirloom is it?"

"Sharp as a tack, you are." Vulgo said. "We picked this off of his daddy after he tried to nab it for himself."

Vick turned slightly to face the others. "That veiled lady—she had one too. It's how she killed all those Rangers."

Talia? Andy remembered, as much as he would have liked to forget. He hoped she was rotting in her cell, after all she had put him through, everything she had done in the name of his 'salvation.' It sickened him to even think she had a passing connection to all this.

Their passing knowledge amused him, but Vulgo was hardly impressed.

"The heirloom can do so much more than kill. It can *hunt*, for instance. It can create," the man chuckled. "It can *control*."

As he said this, the heirloom's energy surged. Vulgo bared his teeth and groaned. Everyone heard what was coming before they saw it—hundreds upon hundreds of kloons descending down the stairs behind them.

Truly, truly trapped, now. The lord laughed as he regained his composure.

"For all this? A memory, some flesh? It's such a trivial thing."

Andy locked onto that glowing amethyst, its pulsing light hypnotically horrifying.

Everything was crystal clear. That amulet wasn't just a weapon, or a simple tool, it was the lynchpin of this entire nightmare. The source of Vulgo's power over the kloons, the key to The Natural Order's schemes. If they could get it away from him, maybe they could turn the tide.

Rex lent his strength to his limbs, and fire to his resolve. Andy launched himself at Vulgo with a snarl, eyes blazing white hot. The sudden attack caught the lord off guard, his laughter cutting. Andy tried to pry the amulet from Vulgo's nasty mitts.

"Get offa me, you mangy mutt," Vulgo said, swinging his free arm in a wide arc. Andy ducked. He could feel the heat of the heirloom, hear its unearthly hum, his fingers brushing against it. Just a little more…

Pain exploded through his side, Vulgo's knee connecting with his ribs. Andy gasped, grip faltering. It was all the opening Vulgo needed. With a bellow, he seized Andy by the throat and lifted him off his feet.

"You *stupid* mongrel," Vulgo sneered, his rancid breath hot on Andy's face. "Did you think I'd let you do that? Did you think it would be easy?"

Vulgo's guards blocked the others from interfering. His grip tightened.

Andy struggled to breathe. His vision began to darken at the edges, all he could hear was his heartbeat slowing down. He wouldn't give up. He couldn't give up. Not with so much at stake.

With the last of his strength, Andy kicked off Vulgo's gut. The man wheezed, his grip failing. The boy jet himself backward, away—off the side of the bridge.

He could hear his father scream his name in utter agony. Not that it mattered, now. They might have been given another chance—for Andy had the heirloom, safe and sound in his hands.

He watched as the light in his peripherals faded to nothing. It was comforting, almost, to be engulfed by the abyss.

But the comfort was fleeting.

Chapter 11

Andy plummeted through the endless void. Forever and ever, it seemed to go on—time had lost its meaning, replaced by the doldrums of anticipation. The boy bode every moment before he inevitably went splat.

But a grisly demise never came—rather, a pinprick of light in his vision, growing larger and brighter with every second. He thought, for a moment, that he had died already. The blinding radiance forced his eyes shut. Weightlessness hit as the light enveloped him completely.

By the time he adjusted to the light, Andy found himself suspended. His momentum came to a stop, dangling high above an alien landscape. Towering mountains of shimmering sand, peaks swirling and iridescent. Before he could soak it in for long, Andy's moment of defied gravity came to an abrupt end. The force shifted, inverted, yanking him downward toward one of the many dunes.

Andy tumbled and rolled down the slope, gritty particles invading his clothes, scratching his skin. Coming to a stop, he spat a mouthful of sand. It was sweet, like powdered sugar mixed with copper aftertaste.

The boy pushed himself up, holding the shoulder which absorbed the brunt of the fall. Every step kicked up a swirling plume of sand, catching the stray light and refracting it into his sensitive eyes. He felt he could see a face in the forming clouds. *Briefly.*

Pale was the sky above, washed out, devoid of clouds and suffused with an eerie ball of light burning miles overhead. Andy came to a stop just as soon as he started walking.

He first verified that the heirloom was on him. Andy examined it with trembling fingers, half-expecting it to blow up after all that. It didn't.

So much trouble over a small thing. He supposed that by now, he should expect catastrophe to come in a tiny package.

Andy quickly pocketed the thing. This war wasn't over yet.

His eyes were drawn now to the large, gaping hole he just came from. He really wasn't expecting to survive that fall. Did he dare attempt to plunge back in? The thought of tumbling through another blackened void made his stomach churn. Another sickening thought came.

Those knights could be here any second, should they be as bold as him. They would be here soon, looking for their heirloom, ready to strike him down.

Perhaps the idea wasn't so far-fetched either, frantic howling could be heard coming his way.

Shooting from the hole, a flailing body, draped in black— Drew, the complete lunatic—he landed face first on the ground.

Andy blinked in disbelief. Had Drew really just come after him? Or had he, too, been tossed off the bridge in the ensuing battle? Suppose he would have an answer soon, as the man came too.

As Andy came into focus, Drew launched himself at the boy and pulled him in for a hug.

"Aw, kid! You're alright! I thought we lost you!"

"Funny, I thought I lost me too." Andy replied.

The two let go, arms falling limp at their sides. At the very least, there was peace enough now to think. Silence was the motif here. No birds chirped, no insects buzzed—even their pounding heartbeats were muffled by the oppressive quiet.

They looked back at the hole, then back at each other. Coming to some mutual agreement in their heads, they both decided to move away in the case of any unwelcome followers.

Plus, in this heat, they would be better off finding shelter, sooner rather than later.

Fairy dust beneath them, Andy and Drew tiredly trudged toward the worn-down cityscape in the distance.

It raised more questions than answers, the closer they got. Any hope of finding shelter was quickly diminished. The desolation here was *apparent*. Scorched sandstone structures that loomed before them were quite sad in shape. Once-proud slabs now crumbled like dirt. There was a faint smoky scent here, though the fires that once raged here long-since died out.

Glassy stalactites stuck out of the ground, explosions frozen in time. Andy wondered if they had always been here, naturally occurring formations, or if they were the result of whatever catastrophe rendered this place lifeless.

The streets, if they could still be called that, were little more than narrow channels between high dunes. Sand reclaimed much of the city. Its few remaining respites looked far too dangerous to dwell beneath for long.

Navigating the dead city was like exploring the fossilized remains of some leviathan creature. Various 'statues' sat half-buried in the sand. Andy didn't recognize the creatures he saw in the glass. Their pointy ears stuck out far past the bounds of their heads. Large, shark-like tails poked out from miniature dunes. Their faces were frozen in anguish. The boy shuddered, averting his gaze from their lifeless eyes. Moving past the crystal remains, the two discovered what they believed to be a library. This building appeared more intact than the rest, and with the false sun beading down on their foreheads relentlessly for the past thirty-or-so minutes…well, they felt a semi-stable shelter was better than none.

Murals on the walls depicted a very different scene to the one outside. Strange, Andy thought, how these colors looked in context. The sky was painted purple, the clouds pink. He mistook the many fluffy trees for an ocean, their leaves painted a deep blue.

Another indecipherable message accompanied the painting, a language long forgotten. Nothing either of them could reasonably read.

The walls eventually transitioned into dust-filled shelves from the mural. Drew was drawn to one display in particular. The object resembled an old-fashioned record player, its brassy horn tarnished, but otherwise all in one piece. Intrigued, he brushed away the cobwebs and lifted the device, surprised by its heft.

Closer to the center of the room was a dusty obsidian pedestal. Drew set the device down there. A rusty crank protruded from the side, begging to be turned. Andy gave it a few rotations, flinching from the discordant screech that subsequently followed.

"Maybe it would work better with a disc, yeah?" Drew asked.

Yeah. Shouldn't be a problem.

Andy rummaged through the nearby shelves with muted excitement. It wasn't long before he unearthed a promising wooden box. Inside, stacks upon stacks of discs, surfaces shimmering after a good wipe from Andy's torn-up sweater. Through years of neglect, these discs looked good as new—it was a relief they hadn't just disintegrated at his touch.

Gingerly, Andy placed one of the discs onto the turntable, holding his breath as he positioned the needle. Drew cranked the device, the disc spun, and a chorus of bells filled the air.

It wasn't like any song he'd heard before. There was a certain cadence to it, a pattern he couldn't quite place. Not *totally* unpleasant, but it definitely rubbed them both the wrong way. Drew's turning of the crank had slowed to a stop.

…What was he doing? How was this old thing going to help him?

They needed a plan, but what plan was there to have right now beyond survival? He needed to get out of this place, but…

Ugh.

Drew sat down on the dark pedestal after kicking up a sizable cloud of dust. He ran his claws through his hair, pushing his bangs out of his eyes over and over. They just kept crashing down. It was *so* aggravating. He about threatened to pull his hair out with a few stiff tugs before he flopped all the way back.

"Don't tell me you're givin' up." Andy said.

"Shut up," said Drew. "I need to think."

Once again, Andy was reminded of the weight in his pocket. With nothing else to guide them, maybe this object could hold... well, *some* kind of answer.

Vulgo did say he could do a lot with it.

Before he knew it, Andy was looking deep into its amethyst center, trying to make out an odd shape.

"Hello, Andrew."

The boy near instantaneously dropped the amulet, allowing for it to hit the ground with a twang.

Drew sat up, looking over. "What was that?"

A quick save. Andy already cupped the amulet in his hands, his back turned to Drew.

"Sorry—I just dropped somethin'." he said.

Drew shook his head and laid back down. "Be careful. This whole place looks like it could fall over from a gust of wind."

There was relief, if not more questions. Drew's inquiry still lingered in the boy's mind. *What was that?* The voice, disembodied, ethereal, didn't come from anywhere in particular. Drew certainly hadn't heard it. No, it's like it was bouncing around inside his own skull.

Hesitantly, Andy focused back on the heirloom. The world around him grew dark. Odd. Andy had the feeling that Drew could no longer hear him—either of them. His words, in this void, were silenced.

"I'm sorry." Andy said. "Was that...*you?*"

The voice came again, clearer this time. "I apologize if I have startled you."

"Who...*what* are you?"

"A guide, of sorts. A presence that resides within this sacred artifact. I have been waiting for quite some time for someone worthy to claim me as their own."

Andy furrowed his brow. "Come again?"

"The fact that you hold this heirloom now proves your worth. Only those worthy can unlock my secrets."

Andy shifted uncomfortably, glancing around the void before his focus came back.

"What kind of secrets? The getting-me-home kind?"

"Of course." the heirloom said. "First, however, you must listen. I can guide you on this path, help you harness the power within you. But all power demands a cost."

Andy nodded, biting his lip. "A memory, right? You want my memories."

"As a sign of faith, perhaps."

The boy's fingers tightened. Part of him wanted to cast it aside at that very moment. Another part of him dreaded his uncertain fate. Elena's face flashed through his mind, along with his foolish promise to keep her safe. Though he was too weak on his own, he wondered if this newfound power could truly make his promises a reality.

"I can sense your yearning, child. Your need to protect those closest to you—embrace me, and no one will threaten you or your loved ones again."

Even as multiple alarm bells sounded off in the back of his mind, the temptation was powerful. He had his reservations, but very few choices.

"Tell me what I need to do."

"There is a great beast that lies dormant in this underworld—to return to your own world, you must seek it out. It lies hidden, deep within the heart of these lands, guarded by what remains of its people."

A great beast? Now this voice was speaking his language. Andy leaned in closer. "Where do I find this beast?"

"First, a small token of your trust. A memory, as discussed—something precious, non-essential."

Andy hesitated. "Ain't too sure there's much precious I'm willin' to part with."

"Sure there is," the amethyst's glow marginally intensified, casting a light across the boy's face. He could feel something prying through his mind. It was something akin to spider legs sifting through the wrinkles of his brain.

A memory came to the surface—his old home, the ranch in Harpers Ferry. He wanted to go back so bad, but deep down, he knew he could never. Imagination ran its course. He saw visions of knights, ransacking the place, leaving it all in ruin. To what extent was the question.

Was that what it hungered for?

Andy wondered just how much of it the entity would take. Would it take the town too? The people, their faces?

Though he's been gone for a long, long time, home was still a part of him. Sentimentality chained him—he was reluctant to give it all away.

His mind squirmed with guilt, sudden, overwhelming, pulsating guilt. Shame of what he'd done to his new home. He was welcomed to this place with open arms, and look where it got them. They're all trapped down here now, the people of Hudsonville, all because Andy had to go and run his mouth. All because he wanted to 'be a real boy.'

The entity pried deeper.

He jeopardized everything for the cure. His friends, his family, all for revenge and some false promise of normalcy after.

It was only a matter of time before The Order attacked again. He should have seen it coming.

Maybe he deserved this.

"Take it." Andy said. "Take it, just...just get me out of this place. *Please*. Help me save my friends."

The heirloom flashed. Andy could feel something like a shard of ice pierce his skull. It clawed its way through, chopping through the folds of his brain like a lawnmower.

A vision of his hometown—he reached out with a trembling hand.

All of it, every last memory, it was all sucked away instantaneously. He wasn't even sure if he had forgotten anything to begin with. Chilling, to say the least.

Blood rushed to his head. Andy's knees buckled. The heirloom nearly fell from his weak hands.

What did he just do?

"Well done, child." the entity said. "Allow me to exchange a memory of my own."

A warmth now caressed Andy's mind, soothing the raw wound. The path stretched before him, as vivid and clear as the memories of his old home.

The trail was long, treacherous, tedious, many miles of shimmering sands between him and his goal. He'd have to navigate past dozens of dry dunes, glassy monoliths, the edges of a dead society.

Through a jagged mountain pass, he would come across a great city, and in that great city, there was...*that thing.*

Whatever creature rested in the heart of the city was difficult to interpret. Every time Andy tried to focus, the memory brought a heavy fog, as if his brain was trying to block out whatever it was he was seeing. Andy opened his eyes, attempting to blink away any thought of the thing at once.

"Okay. Stop. I get it."

He didn't get it. All he knew was that this thing, whatever it was, was far beyond him.

As the vision faded, the voice from the amulet spoke once more.

"Tread carefully as you cross the sands, child. These wastes are not for the faint of heart."

"What do I do if I need you again?" Andy asked.

"I will come to you when the time is right. For now, walk with purpose."

The voice fell quiet. The room came back into focus. Though it had apparently left him, Andy couldn't help but feel like he was still being watched.

Shakily, he slipped the heirloom back into his pocket. Looking behind himself, Drew was passed out on the podium, snoring. The boy approached and woke him up.

"I have an idea," Andy said. "I saw a mountain pass, when I was up in the air. That ought to give us some persistent shade, no havin' to hang around these old buildings."

Drew groaned. Not like they had many options beyond a wild suggestion.

"Whatever you want, kid."

As they stepped back into the light, a presence stirred in the shadows behind.

Long, spindly fingers ending in hooked claws gripped the edge of a broken beam. Three eyes peered from the darkness. They watched with growing malice.

The creature remained still, biding its time, waiting for the perfect moment to strike.

The sound of a rusty bell chimed in its throat.

CHAPTER 12

The walk was long and the desert was dry.

Drier than bone, drier than oatmeal, drier than mom's potatoes.

Dry, dry, dry.

Dryness stretched on for miles.

There was no respite from the dry, nor the heat, and hardly any shade to speak of. Drew almost resented his shorter guide for leading him away from the safe of the city. The false sun beaded on their foreheads. Sweat drizzled down their faces and sizzled on the sand.

Kss. Kss.

Andy wiped his perspiration with a sunburnt forearm. He bit at his parched lips, squinting at the horizon. Not a sign of life. Just how far did these sands stretch on?

He knew the answer already, of course. *Vaguely.*

Uneasy fingers tapped the amulet in his pocket. Andy's head danced with thoughts. He wondered if the entity would be willing to grant him any sage words of wisdom to keep him going.

Perfect timing, then, that they would stumble across some respite up ahead.

A gorgeous blue wavered in the distance, an almost comical oasis of lush trees and crystal-clear springs. Andy blinked, rubbing his eyes, certain it must be a mirage conjured by a dehydrated mind. The closer he stumbled, however, the more the vision solidified.

Fronds of alien trees swayed in a steady breeze that poured from the oasis itself. It was soothing from the moment it touched their reddened skins. The waters sparkled invitingly, surface as smooth as glass. A vibrant array of indigo flora surrounded the spring.

It almost looked obscene, how much it stuck out amidst the harsh, warm tones of the desert.

Passing beneath the shade of the first palm tree, the both of them let out a sigh of relief.

Plump fruit hung from the trees, their skins a deep, glossy purple. They looked *so* juicy. Drew couldn't help but pick one from the lowest hanging branch. The second he took a bite, a savory blend of sweet and tart bathed his tongue. The flesh of the fruit melted like butter. It was unbelievably rich—too rich. He'd need something to wash it down.

At the edge of the pool, Andy was already on his knees, plunging his hands into the deliciously cool water. He brought it to his lips, drinking deeply. Oh, how he relished the feeling. It tasted pure, icy, bubbly, like a freshly cracked can of sparkling water.

Truth be told, the boy was half-tempted to just hop on in after a certain point. Such a thing would soil the perfect purity of his respite, though. He hadn't the heart to defile this place with blood and muck.

Siiiiip. Crunch.

The fatigue that weighed them down whittled away. Strength flowed back into their bodies, the two exchanging positions every now and again. Andy ate, Drew drank. Drew ate, Andy drank. Two and fro, for minutes on end. Even the false sun began to cool, its rays feeling more pleasant than anything.

Andy laid back in the grass, spreading out like a starfish. He breathed in and out. *Haaaah.*

It wasn't all relieving, of course, as he now began to question the convenience of his situation. He really didn't remember this place being here along the way. Though he hoped for an answer from the heirloom, its silent guidance was once more lost on him.

Following his most recent series of unfortunate events, maybe he ought to take this karmic kindness at face value. *Sometimes life throws you a bone,* he thought.

Though this desert stretched on for many more miles, the journey no longer felt as daunting. Still, Andy felt it best to take advantage of the moment. Relaxing, nourishing himself, listening to the winds as they—

Snap.

The sound brought them both back to reality. Drew leapt to his feet. *Where did that come from? The trees? The stones?* The tranquility of their moment shattered, replaced yet again by the sense of unease that's been there from the start.

Drew crept forward, primed and ready. The underbrush rustled as he pushed through. Only around then, he noticed a scent that didn't quite match up to the environment; an odor of soot closer to the ruins than their fresh surroundings. Decay, death, it stuck to his nostrils, making him gag.

At first, he could make out little beyond the vines and leaves. Something was wrong, he just couldn't see it.

Something wrapped itself snug around his ankle. The man looked down, getting a brief glimpse at the smooth appendage before it tore him off his feet.

Drew fell face first into the dirt, dragged backward. He clawed uselessly at the grass, craning his neck to see his attacker. A long, whip-like tail extended from the attacker's spine, coiled still around Drew's leg.

The assailant lunged for his throat, now. Drew rolled to the side, narrowly avoiding the swipe and elbowing the creature in the face. With a hiss, he began to circle Drew, something like a four-limbed serpent. His tail lashed back and forth, stirring up a cloud of dust behind it.

The dust swelled, swirling around Drew in a dizzying, grainy vortex. The haze was far too thick to see through, obscuring anything beyond his shoulder's reach. Awfully hard to breathe, too—every intake came with a mouthful of grit.

Growling, Drew helplessly pawed at the ground. He wanted to get his hands on some kind of weapon, any means by which he could get an upper hand. A few grassy roots, that was a no-go. A fistful of dirt, not likely to do anything. A dry branch blown astray by the wind? *Now that might be worth keeping.*

Drew got back to his feet, readying his improvised weapon like a professional batter, ready to swing.

A dark shape leapt from the cloud. Claws raked across Drew's chest, tearing through both fabric and flesh. He stumbled back with a cry, warm blood seeping into his shirt. The creature lunged again, a flurry of talons. Drew shielded his face, claws scoring his forearms.

Drew swung blindly, the branch connecting with something solid. More importantly, he could feel his weapon snap in half.

The dust cleared up enough for Drew to see what he was at war with;

A tree.

...then where the devil did the—?!

"Oof!"

Drew stumbled as something latched itself onto his back—the creature again, grabbing and pulling at his red mane. It tore out a good few tufts before Drew slammed his back into the battered tree. The creature came right off, though he did not stop his assault. Drew grabbed hold of the creature's wrists this time. His fingers dug in, superhuman strength surging through his arms.

With a snarl, he wrenched the creature's arms to the side. Bones popped, tendons snapped. Drew put his full weight into the throw. The creature spiraled away, tail whipping behind it as it vanished back into the swirling dust. Drew stood panting, his blood siphoning into the parched earth.

A sound rang out, high and lifting and so jarringly out of place. Like the laughter of sleigh bells. As the dust cleared, Drew realized the creature himself was making these sounds, a wide grin spread on his fanged face.

Andy joined Drew's side, putting up his dukes. He may have missed the opening, but he was ready for whatever this hooligan threw at them next.

The creature's form, still obscured by the dust, began to shift and morph. Its skin bubbled and rippled, eyes remaining locked on the boy. Its form filled out, grew broader, taller, angrier, until…

…Until it looked just like Drew.

The same build, the same red hair, the same exact face down to the scars. It was like looking into a living mirror, the only real difference being his eyes. The imposter still bore three distinct eyes, each now matching Drew's hue. The only other difference happened to be their choice of attire. The creature retained its own, a pair of overalls fitted with large bits of scrap metal. Andy thought it looked like something out of Martin's favorite flicks.

The imposter grinned, taking in his new body all the while. He flexed an arm.

"Well, look at that. You had something for me after all."

"You speak English," Drew's eyes narrowed. "Good. I want you to listen up. I've been having a *real* bad day. You don't want to piss me off."

"Hoh," The imposter clapped his hands playfully. "Do not be like that. It is all just a little bit of fun."

"Ain't gonna be fun if you keep pushing."

The creature drew a line in the sand with his toe.

"You do not scare me, surface-one. I would stand to bargain that you could not even cross this line."

"Oh yeah?" Drew snarled. He took a step forward.

Drip. Drip.

Blood oozed his arms at an alarming rate. Those claws had cut much deeper than he initially thought. Drew's vision doubled. He could feel himself about to hurl.

"You little—" Drew fell to one knee.

"As I thought," the doppelganger taunted. "You are soft without all your armor. Easy to bleed."

Andy stepped in front, now. He balled his fists.

"I don't want to fight you." he said.

"Come, now. Do your worst."

"You *don't* want my worst."

"Sure I do."

They walked in a circle, mirroring one another's movements. The false Drew smiled wide and lunged for the fallen.

Andy clumsily redirected the first attack, away from his friend, tackling the imposter to the ground. Another swipe came. He countered with a punch to the creature's face, though he just as easily shrugged it off.

Like animals, the two exchanged wild, dirty attacks. They traded punches and scratches alike, grabbed at each other's hair, kneed each other in the gut. It was all so uncoordinated, so juvenile, so deeply intense.

Andy edged toward the defensive, blocking blows more than he could dish out. He didn't want to give the creature what it wanted, what it so obviously desired—his strength.

But it was very clear the doppelganger had no such reservations. He fought with a killing intent, claws leaving bloody gash after bloody gash across Andy's body. Blow for blow, Andy could barely keep up, his movements growing sluggish by the second. Suddenly, he collapsed.

"Ohh, come now, do not give up just yet," the doppelganger taunted, circling his foe like a shark. Blood pooled around the boy, a moat of crimson.

"You must have it pretty easy on the surface."

Andy could feel it stirring, clawing at the edges of his mind. His alter-ego was at stake here. The fury was beginning to bubble over.

"Maybe when I get there, maybe I will pay your surface friends a visit. I am sure they would not mind the *improvements*."

Andy's eyes blazed. He didn't fight it any more, embracing the rage, letting his fury take hold.

Krraaakkk!

In a painful few seconds, Andy had contorted back into his furry form. Rex's wounds quickly healed. His teeth were bared, his claws sharp as daggers. He rose to his full height, looming over the doppelganger like a wrathful god.

"You want my worst?" Rex asked. "You've got it."

The false Drew's smile only grew wider.

"Well, that is something—"

He was folded instantly by a brutal backhand, courtesy of one beastly bruiser. Rex chased after his prey on all fours as he flew through the air. Just as he threw his next punch, though, a similarly bulky paw had caught it. The creature was shifting forms again, now growing to Rex's height, flashing familiar fangs back at him.

The doppelganger threw a hook into Rex's gut, then snapped at the Werewolf's throat. Rex responded with a heavy left hand, knocking the doppelganger to the floor. The beast took the chance to grab his copy by the scruff, hurling him into a nearby tree. The trunk splintered on impact.

Dazed, the doppelganger gripped the falling tree and pulled upward. Whether it be through adrenaline or sheer brute strength, it managed to get just enough leverage to lift the thing out by the roots and swing it into Rex. The Werewolf crashed through a thicket of barbed bushes. Leaves, petals and thorns flew everywhere, but Rex didn't stay down for long. He came barrelling out from the brush, ready to plunge his claws into the doppelganger's heart.

The two collided. Rex gulped down a breath and slammed his forehead into the other's snout. Something crunched. The imposter staggered, incandescent blood oozing from its nostrils.

An opening.

Rex pressed the advantage, throwing a few hard jabs and off-balance haymakers. The jaw, the ribs, the gut, the doppelganger was forced to endure a bone-shattering onslaught.

One particularly big punch wound up. As soon as Rex swung, the doppelganger's form had shifted yet again—back to his original self.

He hadn't realized it until now, but this creature was quite short at its base. It couldn't have been any more than three feet tall, allowing it to slip beneath Rex's widened stance with ease. A long tail wrapped around Rex's ankles, and like Drew before him, the Werewolf had his legs pulled from beneath him.

Rex landed flat on his stomach. Just behind him, the doppelganger had already shifted back into his bulkier, furrier form. With a running start, he jumped in the air and readied an elbow.

BOUF!

All the wind in Rex's lungs was forced out at once. Before he had time to process this, though, he found himself in a choke hold. His paws fumbled around the hairy arm, trying to pull it away, trying to unbind. All Rex could really think to do was something dirty—a foul play that only heels learned to use—but at that moment, he had no choice. He chose to reach behind himself and give the doppelganger's broken nose a twist.

CRUNCH!

The creature screeched, relinquishing his hold and giving Rex just enough time to escape. Getting to his knees, Rex grabbed hold of the creature's arm, pulled it over his shoulder and tossed him away. It was the doppelganger who had the wind taken out of his sails, now. Just as he managed to recover—

POW!

Rex assaulted the doppelganger with a running dropkick to the chest. He went flying into the deep end of the nearby water. The surface dwellers watched with anticipation.

One bubble, two bubbles, a small cluster of the things raised to the top of the surface; the doppelganger did not.

The bubbles dissipated slowly, one by one.

The doppelganger hadn't resurfaced.

Part of Rex felt a twisted satisfaction. *Let the little twerp suffer, let it choke on the very water it used to lure you in. Death's what he deserves.*

Another part of him felt a scruple of guilt. *As monstrous as this thing was, could you really just stand there and let him drown?*

Rex thought how he'd been given chance after chance. He was scared, confused, he lashed out at anything and everything. It had taken the mercy of another to show him a better way. Without kindness, without forgiveness, where would he be now?

It did kind of look like a kid...

Rex growled, indignant. The waters had grown still, eerily calm. No more bubbles. He had to make a choice now.

The beast dove into the pool.

Cool water soothed his aching muscles, washing the blood from his fur. He swam downward, peering through the depths.

There, at the very bottom, lay the doppelganger in its original form. He'd gone totally limp. As Rex reached to grab the creature, he half expected him to spring to life and drag him down to a watery grave. It remained motionless, though, three eyes glazed over and lifeless.

Rex scooped the doppelganger into his arms and kicked off from the bottom, rocketing back toward the surface. Breaking through with a gasp, he paddled to the shore, precious cargo in tow.

He laid the creature down on the grassy bank, pressing his ear up to the creature's lips. Nothing came. Gritting his teeth, the Werewolf began chest compressions of questionable form. He had never done this kind of thing before, of course, but he had seen it on TV a couple of times. He just hoped that would be enough to translate.

Each compression made the small body jolt. Water dribbled from the corners of its mouth. Still no sign of breathing. Doubt began to creep in. It might have been too late.

After a moment more of trying, Rex gave out a frustrated huff and sat back, giving the creature some space. Suddenly, he began to convulse, his back arching off the ground. He coughed, sputtered, water gushing from his lips.

Rex turned him on his side, letting the fluid drain easier. The creature gasped, drawing in shallow breaths. His eyes blinked open, their depths swelling with confusion.

With a jolt, he scrambled away from Rex, taking cover by the nearby tree. His tail wrapped around himself.

"Y-you," he croaked with a cough. "You *saved* me. Why did you *save* me?"

Rex shrugged. "Dunno. Felt right in the moment."

What sense did that make? The creature scowled.

The beast's fur began to shed, his claws retracting. Andy remained now in the Werewolf's place, looking exhausted. Swallowing bile, the boy took a seat at the edge of the water.

"Plus, I reckon I could use your help."

"My help?" the creature asked.

"I don't plan on stickin' 'round down here for long, an' I figure you ain't a fan of this place either."

The creature went quiet, processing. Sure, that made sense. A surface dweller would probably have better chances of surviving down here with a friend. The only problem; *friendships with surface dwellers hardly lasted long.*

Andy reached a hand out, a placating gesture.

"My name's Andy. What's yours?"

The creature hesitated, then a short, sad jingle came from its lips. Andy looked a bit confused.

"I'm sorry?" Andy repeated.

The creature shrugged. "You can just call me Dink."

"What are you?"

Dink deliberated on the question for a moment, taking Andy's hand.

"I am a Changeling. Most down here are."

"Do you have a settlement?"

Dink nodded and pointed off toward the distance. "Through the mountain pass."

"That's right where we're headed, actually," Andy said. "Y'all got a *great beast* or somethin', right?"

The Changeling choked up a bit. He stared at Andy suspiciously, mind racing with the implications. Drew, too, looked rather confused.

"Great beast?" the man asked.

"I hear it's our only chance of gettin' out of here." Andy continued.

"Uhuh? And *who* did you hear that from, exactly?"

"You do not know what you are asking," Dink said before Andy could respond. "That *thing* is long dead. You better hope it stays that way."

"I ain't got much of a choice. We can't stay down here."

"Then you are bigger fools than I took you for."

A sad jingle sounded from Dink's lips. He turned and started pacing away, though he stopped after just a few steps. His lips were pursed.

"You want to go back, why? You are not like any surface person I know. What's so good about the surface for beasts such as yourselves?"

"The Humans got us up against a wall, but…I mean, we got a pretty nice home, up there. It's…" Andy's brows furrowed. "…the only home I've ever known."

"What would you say are the chances they would take someone like me?"

"Pretty high."

"And our great beast? You say it is a way out?"

"Potentially."

"'*Potentially?*' Andy, what are you talking about?" Drew asked. Andy sheepishly pulled out the heirloom. Drew's face paled.

"*Oh.*"

Dink rubbed his chin. He eyed the heirloom with cautious optimism.

"I think I like our odds." he said.

CHAPTER 13

Andy, Dink and Drew continued through the scorching heat, the arid breeze whipping at their faces. As they crested a towering dune, the pair caught sight of another city, long abandoned.

Its towers looked about ready to crumble, its many buildings weathered and brittle. Once-proud spires loomed, bent out of shape, deformed, on the brink of collapse. Their walls were poked with gaping holes and innumerable tiny divots. Shards of colored glass littered the ground around them.

They stepped into the cool shade of one interior, giving themselves a break from the sun.

"Agartha was once ruled over by the Fae, or so they say," said Dink. "Emperor Twiggly established a utopia, right here, in the heart of it. This city was also, supposedly, the birthplace of the Changelings," Dink sighed. "Our world was beautiful."

"What happened?" Andy asked.

"The Humans did," said Dink. "They came down well over a century ago, led by one of our own. They brought destruction. Everything the Fae built over thousands of cycles was flattened in moments."

Andy listened close, his hand unconsciously drifting to his pocket. The artifact pulsed warmly, responding to the tale being told.

Dink took note, of course.

"They used an amulet, just like the one you have. They used it to nearly wipe us out, all of us. I thought you were one of them, coming to finish what they started."

The heirloom felt heavier, somehow. Andy's head lowered, imagining a time where this city wasn't so desolate.

"I'm sorry." he said. "I had no idea."

Dink shrugged. "Don't worry about it. *You* are not a maniac, at least. How did you get your hands on that thing, anyways?"

"It's a long story. Back where I'm from, we was attacked by some fellas callin' themselves The Natural Order. They sent in a whole legion of kloons to our home, an' stuffed us in their hive."

"Kloons?" Dink asked.

"Yeah, they're like these little puffballs with…with *sharp teeth*."

"You mean…?" *Jingle, jingle.* A question posed, but Andy couldn't discern what it was. Dink hardly contained his smile. "No. You could not possibly mean that."

"I know it sounds ridiculous, but that's the truth. When there's a horde of them things comin' after you, it ain't no laughin' matter."

Dink laughed loudly, in fact. The other two swore they felt the building shake.

"What's so funny?" Drew asked.

"'Kloons' are not scary. They are *food*."

Andy blinked.

"What?"

"You heard me. They are uh, *hmm*, actually pretty hard to find here these days. I would go as far as to consider them a delicacy."

"You *eat* kloons?"

"Why would we not? Kloons are full of sugar, Changelings need sugar," Dink waggled his shoulders, as if trying to squeeze in a *'you know.'*

"I guess it sounds pretty silly when you put it like *that*," Andy said. "There was thousands of 'em, though."

"Well if there were that many of them, maybe I could see it," Dink gestured with his pinky. "One of my cousins got his finger bit off by a kloon."

"They'll do more than take a finger, they tore our friend to shreds," Andy pulled out the heirloom. "The Order was controllin' 'em somehow, usin' this thing."

Drew found himself eyeing it, Dink too. Andy continued.

"I don't get his plan—Vulgo's. He's *completely* nuts. Wants to make Humans stronger usin' us folk somehow. He's got all my friends trapped, too."

"Right." Dink said. "A time-sensitive quest, this is, yes?"

"Yeah. We'd better keep movin'."

"Question." Drew said.

"Uhuh?"

"If you've got the amulet now, how's The Order controlling the kloons?"

Andy paused. That was a pretty good question. How would they carry out their plans without it? Worse yet, what would the kloons do while not under their control?

A rumble shook the earth beneath their feet. Dust and debris pelted them from the crumbling ceiling. Andy looked around in alarm, but Dink quickly put a hand to the boy's shoulder, and shook his head. After a long moment of quaking, and waiting, the ground steadied.

"What was *that?!*" Andy asked.

"Sandworm." Dink said. "Pretty common around here. We are going to have to find a *speedy* before we head out."

The Changeling immediately started snooping around. The meticulous rhythm of opening doors rang around in the room, Andy left to gawk.

"A speedy…?" his twisted, bewildered. "*Sandworm?!* You can't just be saying these things."

"Sandworms—big worms. They feel for vibrations in the sand. We do not want that. A *speedy* will let us fly *over* the sand, thus, no sandworms."

"Do we need to be worried about them right now?" Drew asked.

"While we are in the city, no, not really. The foundations here should keep them out of the limits. Anywhere *past* that..."

"Okay."Andy said. "What are we looking for, exactly? A *speedy*? Is it like a bike, a hoverboard, what?"

"I do not know what any of those things are."

"Okay. What does it look like?"

"Long, flat, big wings on the sides."

Made about as much sense as everything else.

"Let's get started then." Andy said.

Objective in mind, the three ventured back into the blistering heat. They walked through the cross-hatched streets, past salty pillars, a few busted shops, a large open plaza; arriving in front of what appeared to be a grocery store, scattered across the sand-strewn pavement of the 'parking lot' were the rusted husks of several 'speedies.'

They were about what Dink had described—flat, ovoid, made up of some sort of brass. Some had small railings on the sides, and clear spots to plant one's feet. There were stylized wings bolted onto the sides of some vehicles, but most were long-since missing the addition.

Dink approached the nearest one. The paint had since peeled, the sheen scratched away by the wind and sand. He ran a hand along the chassis, brushing away the excess dust. Deft fingers pried open a panel and rearranged a snag of colored wires.

"You sure you know what you're doin'?" Andy asked.

"Yup," Dink said, shooting a grin back. "I mess with engines a lot, back at the settlement."

Spark, spark.

The device coughed once two wires touched. It purred with life, sands rippling around it. Dink turned around and pointed to another one of the scrapped vehicles.

"Do you mind grabbing the steering stick off of one of those?" he asked. Drew got to work, looking for whatever he could interpret as a 'steering stick.' He figured it must have been the lever jutting out from the scrap-vehicle's center. It looked to be fused to the vehicle, though. Drew wasn't sure how to remove it.

"Hey, uh, how do I go about this?" he asked.

"Just pull it out, it is not alchemy."

Drew gave it a pull. No luck.

"It's stuck."

"Gods, let me do it," Dink groaned. He approached, one of his arms taking the shape of Rex's. With one swift and jerky motion, he liberated the lever from its prison, a mass of wires being torn like roots from underneath. He then slipped the lever into the humming speedy's empty socket.

Pulling back on the lever, the vehicle lifted a few feet into the air. Dink let out a whoop, steadying the speedy like a pro. He tapped the space behind him with his foot.

"Okay, hop on! Next stop is my home."

Fear of worms fresh in his mind, Andy hesitated. The speedy shifted under his weight, only adding to his fears. Regardless, he set himself behind Dink, gripping tightly onto the metal rails. Drew followed, lacking about as much grace.

Dink pulled his goggles down and pushed the lever forward, the speedy taking off. Wind whipped past Andy's hair, velocity picking up drastically in a matter of seconds. The surface dwellers felt sick, zipping back and forth around the ruins. The city shrunk behind them, whereas the jaws of the mountain pass steadily grew.

Dunes, dunes and more dunes. Nothing worth writing home about, beyond a few odd dust storms in the distance. Funny enough, they seemed to be heading in the duo's direction. Andy frowned.

"Y'all get dust bowls 'round here?" he asked. "And can this thing go any faster?"

Dink blinked, looking off toward whatever Andy had been staring at.

Oh no. The Changeling's eyes bulged. He leaned as far into the steering stick as he could manage. The speedy sped ahead.

Andy and Drew struggled not to fall off.

"What's wrong?!" Andy said.

"Raiders," said Dink.

"*Raiders?*" Drew asked.

As the clouds got closer, Andy could spy the mass at their centers—more speedies, with Changeling riders. They didn't look too friendly.

"I hope you brought some firepower!" Dink said.

He already knew the answer to that, but Andy still patted his pockets. Nothing but the smooth surface of the heirloom—its warmth pushed through the fabric. Other than *that*, he was empty-handed.

Dink white-knuckled the steering stick. The raiders closed in fast, false sunlight shining off the barrels of their weapons—makeshift mixes between rifles and crossbows. A barrage of energy bolts rained down around their prey, surrounding sands exploding into trees of crystal. The earth rumbled.

"Hold on!" Dink said. He jerked the steering stick hard to the left. The speedy banked sharply, nearly throwing its passengers off. A sizzling bolt whizzed past Drew's ear, close enough to singe his hair.

The speedy dipped and weaved, occasionally skimming the surface of sand. Soon came the low rumblings of before. Andy watched as wave-like patterns swam across the dunes. Something big just woke up.

Dink pushed the machine to its limits, engine roaring. Sand sprayed out behind them in a cloud, obscuring some raiders from view. Andy could still hear their violent bells, carried by the wind.

Something else overpowered the sound, the screaming, the roar of the engine—the subsequent eruption of earth.

Easily over a hundred feet long, a segmented body exploded out from the sand and into the sky above. Its shovel-like face aimed down, pointed directly at the struggling speedy. Dink took another sharp turn. The others held on tight.

The sandworm crashed down into the dunes, taking out a trailing raider in the process. Its massive jaws snapped shut with a sickening metallic crunch; the Changeling only had a second to scream.

Drew was about as calm as the ill-fated stranger.

"What the hell was *that?!*"

"Sandworm," Dink called behind. "Let us hope we do not get too intimate!"

"*What?!*"

"Hold on!"

Dink angled the speedy back toward the dueling peaks of the pass. The raiders followed close behind, bolts chipping away at the rock face. Once more, the sandworm's huge body corkscrewed through the dunes and into the air. Its maw opened wide.

The stray heroes flew, above jagged rocks, tight around deadly pitfalls. They ducked their way into the narrow canyon. The sandworm's roar echoed behind. Its body whipped back and forth, slamming into the canyon walls. Large stones, unmoved by the centuries, began to crumble.

Dink juked the speedy to the side, narrowly avoiding a falling boulder. Behind them, the trailing raiders weren't so lucky. Their speedies collided with the tumbling rock, exploding into fiery bursts of shrapnel and smoke. A few remaining pursuers pressed on.

Andy was being pushed to the edge. It was entirely too much for him, everything. He tried to get his bearings, to ground himself on something, but it was all too noisy, too chaotic.

All beyond the heirloom.

The amulet pulsed with insistent heat, whispers worming their way into Andy's ears.

"You know what to do, child," the voice spoke softly in his mind. "Embrace me. My power can save you."

There wasn't much time to think about it. Another bolt whizzed by and struck the front end of the speedy. It dipped and scraped against the ground, sparks flying. The sandworm was once more given notice of their location.

Andy unpocketed the heirloom, steady as he could to not drop it. He could feel its energy thrumming through his palm. It was tantalizing, the temptation, overwhelming. Something else filled his mind—something like instinct, telling him to aim the heirloom at whatever needed breaking.

As he did so, the amethyst at the center surged with a blinding light. Like his mind before, it felt as though icicles were being shot through Andy's hand. He watched as his veins began to glow with that same magenta, the light slowly spreading up his arm. It was a fire so hot, it nearly looped back around to being cold.

The inner voices grew to a crescendo, urging him to unleash whatever it was he had built up. Thrusting his hand forward, a bolt of cosmic energy was sent past a raider's head and into the canyon wall. The rock shattered like glass, boulders the size of houses breaking free in a cataclysmic avalanche. They, the raiders, had no time to react. Their speedies were crushed beneath the falling stone, small bodies pulverized in an instant. Fireballs erupted from the wreckage, painting the canyon in lurid shades.

Dink let out a whoop, rocketing away from the collapse. The sandworm behind roared in frustration, path blocked by the mounting rubble. Andy slumped into Drew's arms, energy spent. His fingers had blackened, the skin on his arm smoking.

He risked a glance behind, noting the sandworm's pause.

For a moment, Andy thought they may have lost it, but such hopes were dashed as the damaged speedy continued to scrape at the ground. The creature's head swiveled. It reared up and burrowed into the sand.

The speedy's underside once more grazed the earth. Andy yelped. Drew cussed. Dink made a noise like a cowbell, fighting to keep control of the stick. He pulled back hard, gaining just a bit of altitude. The vehicle groaned in protest.

"Come now, come now...!" Dink growled.

The worm's face rose to the surface, dangerously close to their backsides. Its maw opened wide, ready to engulf them. Dink howled his lungs out as he pulled back on the lever, more and more until—

SNAP!

A bit too hard. The stick was yanked out of its socket, and Dink went flying backward. He knocked Andy right off the back of the speedy, and consequently onto the sandworm's flat head. Drew hopped off to join the others aboard the creature. With no way of saving it, the vehicle careened downward, right into the beast's mouth.

Satisfied, the sandworm began to lower its head again. Earth approached fast—the three had to make a decision fast.

Andy took note of two flaps on the creature's back, hot breath steaming out from beneath. About to be submerged, the flaps shut tight.

Nostrils?

"Sorry about this, big fella." Andy said.

He grabbed the broken lever from Dink's shaking hands, and jammed it between the flaps. With a heave, he forced them upward. The creature bellowed in annoyance, surfacing once again. Furious now, it began to thrash. Each movement threatened to fling the trio into the rocks.

"This is *insane,*" said Drew.

"You're tellin' me!" Andy replied.

Holding on for dear life, the three spotted something up ahead—a scrapyard city, precariously spanning the gap of canyon walls like a bridge. The hazardous construct would have garnered several health code violations upstairs, but down here, to Andy? It looked like salvation.

Bells rang out from the city as several Changelings noticed the commotion below. They gestured wildly to each other, pointing at the raging sandworm and its unwilling riders. After some frantic activity up above, a rope ladder unfurled from the city's center. It dangled oh-so-tantalizingly close up ahead.

Andy swallowed, trying to keep his heart from hopping up into his throat. The ladder swayed, one good jump out of reach. The boy psyched himself up, his legs danced abord the creature. On the count of three, he'd let go of the lever and leap.

One...

Two...

Andy clenched his eyes shut.

Three.

The boy launched himself up into the air, just as the rope ladder seemed to pass him by.

He missed his opportunity. Andy's hand remained outstretched for a heart-stopping second.

Like a cracking whip, Dink's tail wrapped around Andy's wrist—seems as though the Changeling managed to make it, where Andy fell short. He dangled from the ladder with a relieved look on his face. Drew was just above him, refusing to look down.

"Good news," said Dink.

Drew swallowed. "Just tell me you got him."

Andy watched as the massive creature passed below, burrowing its way back into the earth. All the color drained from his face by the time he looked back up.

"Thank you." he squeaked. Drew let out a sigh of relief.

The Changelings above cheered and began hauling up the ladder, hand over hand. Dink clung to the rungs tight, Andy to his tail. The canyon walls slowly fell away to a dizzying view.

Dozens of eager hands reached out to help them onto solid ground. Drew landed first, Dink following, then Andy, the boy's legs weak.

The sound of bells was deafening, but grew quiet as more and more heads turned toward the castaways. Dozens stared with wide eyes. The two surface dwellers shuffled uncomfortably under the scrutiny, like specimens being put under a microscope.

One by one, the Changelings' forms blurred, their features rearranging like clay. Within moments, Andy found himself surrounded by a sea of his own face. Drew experienced more or less the same thing on his side of the aisle.

Each Changeling was akin to a distorted reflection, like they found themselves inside a house of mirrors. Some of their ears were a bit too long, their noses a bit too sharp. Some of them had three eyes, some had four. Some had gangly limbs. Some were much too short.

He could understand what they were all saying now, too, he realized. The once incomprehensible chimes had taken on meaning, and he was bombarded with a choir of his own voice.

"Surface dwellers?"

"Why did he bring a surface one?"

"They do not belong here!"

"What do they want?"

A heated debate ensued, the two strangers growing uneasy. Dink held his hands up, his own rusted jingle cutting above the rest. The crowd continued to argue, but as Dink explained, they started to quiet down, listening. Whatever he was saying seemed to work.

The sea of distorted faces shifted, from confused to awestruck. The lot of them stared back at Andy, heads tilting, curiosity piqued. Some dispersed, a few of them waving to And as they reverted to their natural forms. The boy blinked, waving back, unsure. Many stook around to really get a good look at him.

"I'm guessin' this is a good thing." Andy said. "What did you tell them?"

"Not much, just that you saved my life."

Tug, tug. Andy turned to see a broad-shouldered Changeling, half his height, offering some fresh desert clothes. The boy raised a brow.

"Is that *all* you told them?"

"I might have asked for a few favors. Get dressed and we can go eat."

Andy nodded, the wide Changeling gesturing for him to follow. Doing so, the group ended up in a tiny tin house. They were given just enough privacy to freshen up. Andy threw the poncho-like cloth over his head and stuffed his arms into the sleeves. The cuffs barely reached his wrists, and when he tried on the pants, the legs rode high above his ankles. Drew, seeing just how small the garbs were, opted against the change of clothes.

Still, Andy was thankful to have something fresh to wear after having nothing but sloppy, torn-up rags for a good stretch. He emerged from the home to find Dink waiting for them both. A few wandering Changelings stuffed their faces with something deep-fried. Andy's mouth watered.

"You look well, surface one." Dink said.

"Thanks," Andy said, eyes trained on the food. "Where'd they get that?"

"Mess hall." Dink said. "Come now, this way."

The three made their way across the sheet-metal sanctuary. Shoddily-constructed walkways, creaking homes, Andy wondered how it all stayed together for so long. A few stalks of sugarcane were planted in a rooftop garden, casting a truss-like shadow down below.

They came across a large, open building, clouds of smoke billowing from its aluminum chimney. A savory aroma embraced the two outsiders like an old friend, almost smothering. Andy felt like he was going to pass out if he didn't chow down soon.

Dink showed them to the end of the line, grabbing a bowl and a pronged instrument along the way. As they waited, Andy noticed a few of the Changelings still staring at him. Again, he couldn't help but wonder what Dink had told them, expecting a lot more resistance. After all, they *were* outsiders, taking resources away from this *clearly* struggling community. Why did everyone suddenly seem so neutralized, so...*enamored?*

He had a feeling he wasn't going to be getting any straight answers from the Changeling any time soon. Still, Dink helped out a great deal already. Maybe there really wasn't anything to be worried about.

The boy skewered his mysterious fried food once he sat down and raised it to his mouth.

Crunch. Ptooey!

The taste which assaulted his tongue was not one he expected. It was like burnt sugar—sugar that was breaded, battered and deep fried into an unrecognizable mess. It was an attack on sugar and everything it held dear, blasphemy to the sweetest degree.

Andy looked up to Dink, who was slovenly slurping down fried sugar like a racehorse. His nose wrinkled in disgust, watching every greasy drop dribble down the Changeling's chin. Once he was finished, Dink licked his lips and eyed Andy's hardly-touched 'food.'

"Are you going to eat that?" Dink asked.

Andy sighed, pushing the bowl forward.

"Knock yourself out."

CHAPTER 14

Darkness. Nothingness. Emptiness.

So blissful to be asleep, no matter the context. Andy's consciousness drifted back and forth, floating along like a leaf in the breeze.

The first sensation he felt was a dull throb in the back of his skull. *Throb, throb,* like a tiny drummer was swatting at his spine with tiny mallets.

Light. Everything. Too much.

A pinprick had pierced his eyelids, quickly spreading, flickering incessantly. Like someone was strobing a flashlight. Groggily, Andy blinked against the warm glow of a fire.

Something else was there, in the corner of his vision—a trio of eyes, staring back at him.

"Hey, you." Dink said. "Feeling healthy?"

Andy sat up, massaging his neck and shoulder. *Where was he?* After him and Dink ate, they were shown to their 'quarters,' and… right. The community bedroom. Not even two seconds of resting and he had fallen asleep.

He looked around at the dozens of other cots surrounding his own, most of them sporting some manner of sleeping Changeling.

"I s'pose." Andy said. "What's up?"

"It is time." said Dink.

"For?"

"For you to commune with the beast. Is that not what you were here for?"

"I…guess, but—"

"Shh. The others *cannot* know about this. Come now, we must go."

Andy hesitated. He didn't want to get in any more trouble, but Dink was probably right. This *was* his goal from the beginning. Suppose it didn't matter what his mind meandered on—his legs already carried him in his new friend's direction.

Drew, miraculously, was still sound asleep. Andy debated waking him, but, something in his gut told him to let sleeping dogs lie.

The two quietly stepped out into the quiet settlement, Dink flinched at every squeak made by the rusty floors. All was still, save for the waving of a few banners. Dink took the liberty of grabbing one.

Despite the false sun shining on as always, Andy figured *everyone* must have some sort of cycle. Even the local livestock had settled in for the evening—large birds Andy had sworn had gone extinct centuries ago.

A jagged cave entrance waited for the two at the edge of the settlement. Dink, wrapping the stolen banner around its base, set it ablaze with some form of lighter he produced from his pocket. The makeshift torch cast a warm glow on Andy's face.

"It is a long way in." Dink said. "Are you prepared?"

A nod, Andy's lips pressed together. Dink grinned and stepped into the cavern.

"I will admit, I have been curious, myself, for quite some time. 'Never go in there,' the elders will say. 'Never stir what lies beneath.'"

It stretched on, and on, bending, curving, the boys having to climb a good amount of the way. The walls glistened, the air was damp. Andy felt as though he was lugging around an extra twenty pounds of weight.

"But this has been on my mind for quite some time, yes, quite some time. I always knew there was more beyond the desert. But always, always, they tell you not to stray. Well not any longer."

Soft protrusions brushed by the two's ankles, leaving traces of slime. A few membranous walls had to be broken through by hand. Andy felt no satisfaction removing them.

The boys eventually happened upon a large, loose-looking slab in the wall, nestled in behind a growth of tendril-like plants.

"This is it." Dink said. "Can you help me move the door?"

"That's a door?" Andy asked.

"Yes, smart boy, it is a door, now help me move it."

Andy rolled his shoulders, pressing on the bottom where Dink held his hand. Dink slipped underneath and swapped forms, holding the door open for Andy to come through. Once they were both inside—

WHUMP.

The slab was allowed to slam shut. The noise caught Andy off guard, getting him a bit turned around before he wound up face-to-face with his imposter. Dink smiled.

"We are here."

Andy realized just what they were standing under.

It was difficult to tell at first, what with all the giant wrinkles and bumps. Its surface was mottled, deep with furrows and ridges that gently pulsated with a dormant energy. The air around them hummed. Andy could feel his whole body vibrate.

Dink's meek torch hardly penetrated far enough through the dark to get a good idea of how large the organ was. It must have been the circumference of several football fields, a colosseum-sized tumor hanging from the stone.

It was a giant brain. A giant, pulsating, slimy brain.

Andy had just about snapped, seeing it. He could feel the hot sting of bile rising in his throat, doing everything in his power to make sure it didn't come up.

The heirloom hummed again. Andy dug it out without hesitation. It had better provide him with a reasonable explanation.

But there was nothing. Not a peep.

It was frustrating, although…Andy noticed the light of the heirloom reacting to his arm's lateral movement. Steadying his hand, he slowly pointed the amulet upward. Immediately, he could feel a tethered connection establish, an invisible strand connecting mind-to-mind.

The voice returned.

"Good. You are close, child. Now, focus your thoughts. Find me another *memory*, something that has shaped you."

Icy tendrils burrowed once more into Andy's mind. The world around him dissolved into a dark mist, the giant brain and Dink's face fading to nothing.

A new scene took vague shape, never reaching clarity.

Everything was blurry, molten, like a watercolor painting left out in the rain. Indistinct shapes and colors swirled together into a hauntingly familiar landscape.

Like a spotlight cutting through the haze, two figures, clear as day, emerged from around a smudged corner. Martin, looking rough and tough as usual, and then…

Miriam. Mom.

It shocked Andy to see her again. Miriam looked just as she had before. The woman's greying bob draped above her shoulders, perfectly framing the warm expression on her face. She looked so *real*.

Andy's lips trembled. He tried to speak, but nothing came of it. He tried to reach out to Miriam, but his hand was invisible. The boy did not exist here, in this memory, not as he was at the moment at least. No, instead, a slightly younger version of himself came walking in the door, greeting Miriam with a hug. His Human self, or at least, how he remembered it.

His face was a bit off, almost like a reflection. The present Andy supposed that's how he knew himself best.

"Hey, hun," Miriam said as she ran a hand through his hair. "How'd it go? Any assignments?"

"Nothin' yet." said the reflection. "Just a lot of curr-ic-u-lum. Ground rules."

"See, if it were up to me, you'd be doin' multiplication tables day one," Martin piped in from behind his newspaper.

The reflection laughed and rolled his eyes. "That's like… third grader stuff."

"Right, you're a 'big kid' now, ain't you?"

"Big enough to go to an actual school."

Miriam scoffed. "We didn't do that bad of a job, did we?"

"We'll see," the reflection said with a shrug.

Andy got a bad feeling. He craned his head toward the amulet. "Why are you showing me this?"

"Because you must make a decision. Which one do you value more?"

The boy paused. "You *can't* be serious."

"*Deathly,*" the voice whispered. "Choose. Whom will you surrender in exchange for my aid?"

"No," Andy shook his head. "No way, no how. I can't…I can't lose either of them."

"Then you are content to *die* down here, while your friends are left to die up above?"

"There has to be another way."

"Is there? You are alone. You are without willing peers. It is you against hordes of man and monster. You are outmatched."

"The Rangers will help them."

"I wouldn't be so sure. The labyrinth which spreads beneath your town is *unfathomable*. Why would you leave their fates up to chance? And what of your father? Your friends? Are you to break their hearts and remain buried?"

Andy's grip tightened. The voice continued to dig.

"You're a selfish boy, aren't you? Clung to the past while those who care for you now suffer. Your father already made the necessary sacrifice. He understood the weight of his actions."

"What? He's dealt with you, too?"

"Of course he has. How do you think he found you? Where do you think he got the power to save you? He knew the cost, and he paid it willingly."

"He...he forgot about Mom?"

"For you. To protect you. To keep you safe."

Each word was like a barbed arrow. Struggle as he might, he couldn't tear them out. They lingered, bleeding him dry, his ability to make rash decisions skyrocketing.

"Your mother is gone. *Nothing* will change that. But your father, your friends, they still draw breath. They have a chance, should you have the courage to do what must be done."

Tears stung Andy's face. An awful ache built in his stomach.

"I...*can't*. Please. There has to be another way."

"There is no other way. This is the path you've chosen. The only question is, will you see it through?"

The aching built to a crescendo, his heart, his lungs, his ribs feeling tight, each breath burning. It was all his fault, it was. This was the price he had to pay to be happy, to be content. He didn't want to follow through on it, he didn't want to allow this thing to consume him.

But for the briefest moment, Andy had a lapse. He really, truly believed, even if it was only for mere seconds, that this was the correct choice.

He looked at his mother again, committing every detail to memory one last time. The way her eyes were forced shut when she smiled. The faint wrinkles on her forehead. Her absurd earrings. Her deep brown eyes.

The warmth of her embrace. The smoothness of her voice.

"I'm sorry," he said, voice cracking. "I'm so sorry."

His hand shaking, Andy raised the amulet yet again, the connection between it and the brain now crackling with an intense light. He focused on the memory, on the face, and with a blood-curdling cry, he let it all go.

The memory shattered like glass, sucked into the void. Andy nearly fell to his knees, wracked with sobs which quickly died out, as he no longer remembered what exactly he had lost.

What an empty feeling.

The brain pulsated, faster and faster, throbbing with light. Andy and Dink were bathed in a foreign glow, a color they had not recognized. A deep heartbeat filled the chamber, louder and louder. The air vibrated in time with the rhythm. The 'cave' shook. The walls softened and breathed.

This 'great beast' did not dwell within the mountain.

It *was* the mountain.

The jagged peaks, the craggy slopes, all that had towered before him as he approached for hours on end…they were not formed by geological forces. The giant pass he had approached was merely the slacked jaws of some ancient superorganism, waiting, half-buried in the sand with baited breath.

Andy could sense the stirring of a vast, alien consciousness, a mind so ancient and powerful that it defied his comprehension.

The ridges and furrows that lined the brain's surface rippled. They flowed in hypnotic patterns, dancing spasms.

Dink stood transfixed on the sight.

"Behold, child," the voice echoed in Andy's mind. "You stand in the presence of a demigod—an entity that has witnessed the birth and death of countless creatures, the rise and fall of several civilizations, the ebb and flow of reality itself. Through your hands, you have earned its favor. Its power is now yours to command."

Ahead of Andy, an illusory veil began to form, almost like a giant TV screen. Upon it was a vision of the landscape they had recently trekked, now from the perspective of the great beast. Everything looked so small now.

Andy shivered. Fear, sadness, a bit of confusion, his mind raced with thoughts. He took a deep breath to steady himself.

Raising the pulsing heirloom high, he issued one simple command with his mind;

Forward.

A guttural rumble shook the chamber, the ground beneath their feet pitching and heaving. Dink let out a yelp and grabbed onto Andy's leg for support.

With thunderous cracks, the earth split. Gargantuan, stone-encrusted arms burst from the ground, geysers of sand and rubble sent high into the air. House-sized boulders were flung into the nearby abandoned cities, smashing them to dust.

Dink watched with slacked-jawed horror as the titan hauled its bulk from the earth. Every single shuddering motion unleashed seismic waves across the landscape. Clouds of grit billowed in its wake, blotting out the false sun and casting a ruddy shadow.

In the distance, the massive hole the boys initially came from looked...*smaller*. Where it once appeared to be miles away, it now only looked to be within a few paces.

The titan took a step forward, its legs diving deep into the ground. More debris was sent flying, more shockwaves permeated the earth. Towers crumbled beneath the onslaught of debris. Temples and palaces were reduced to further rubble. A number of sandworms wriggled away from the giant that threatened to crush them. To Andy's horror, even their earlier oasis was on the move. It sprouted stubby legs, barely sidestepping the behemoth.

He tried to ignore all the wanton destruction as they progressed toward the hole. Each massive step brought him a bit closer to home, after all. For the moment, Andy looked down to his Changeling companion.

Dink clung to Andy, his chest heaving, sweat draining down the sides of his face. His eyes twitched. Andy felt for the kid, of course—

he must be terrified, terrified that his whole city might have been crushed inside this thing's mouth. And what about Drew?

If anything, they at least had to have had enough time to evacuate right? He could only hope.

The titan shuddered and groaned and bent its knees at the cusp of the hole.

Down, Andy commanded.

It began to lower itself into the abyss. The walls of the chasm rushed past. Andy did his best to steady his own breathing. He and Dink walked along the walls as gravity continued to shift. Things felt heavier here.

Amidst the eerie thump of its heartbeat, another noise caught Andy's attention—shouts, screams, a choir of voices rising. It came from the other side of the skull flap.

The others—Andy felt a wave of calm, but not for long before something else took hold—*dreadful guilt.*

Dink must have felt it too, looking pale as ever.

"They do not sound pleased," he said.

"They sound pissed." Andy replied. *Gulp.* "What do we do?"

"I will handle them," Dink squared his shoulders. "You keep this *thing* going where it needs to go. Get us out of here."

The Changeling's form rippled into a near-perfect copy of Rex. He strode toward the skull flap, pushing his weight up against it.

Andy turned his attention back to the task at hand. He closed his eyes, focusing on the heirloom. Its power shot through his veins.

Upward, he commanded, willing the titan to climb. *Hurry.*

Andy braced himself against the wall, the titan ascending at a steady rate. The shouts on the other side of the skull flap continued amidst the rumbling. He could only imagine the anger they must be feeling.

There was no turning back now. They had to press on, return to the surface, to his friends, to the world he knew.

The shouting grew louder, more frenzied. The Changelings' rage was felt by all parties. Dink stood firmly against the pressure, but even in Rex's powerful form, the others' fury lent them unnatural strength.

Inch by inch, the skull flap began to buckle. Dink's muscles trembled, snout contorted. The flap splintered, and a sea of grasping hands burst through, clawing at Dink. In a flash, his form melted away, back to his true self. He couldn't risk the others getting a hold of Rex's strength—but without his strength, Dink was no match for the horde.

They spilled into the titan's skull like a plague of locusts, faces twisted with rage, with despair, with pure contempt. The same power that was used to bring ruin to their people, once more used to steal their respite, to destroy their last bastion of hope.

At least Drew was safe among them, he, too, looking utterly bewildered.

"*You,*" one of them hissed, jabbing a finger toward Andy. "We should have known not to trust you!"

"I'm sorry!" Andy said. "I really didn't think this was how this was going to go."

"That is the problem with you surface creatures, you do not think!"

"You're *absolutely* right, and I'm sorry," Andy cleared his throat. "But I promise y'all, this ain't as bad of a deal as you might think—"

"We are *well* past thinking, surface boy. Now is the time to act."

Andy raised the amulet with a trembling hand, eldritch light cast across the Changeling's angry features.

"Stay back!" Andy said. "I don't want to hurt you."

Fury was a powerful force, however. The Changeling rushed forward, readying their claws.

The amulet pulsed, its power singing Andy's skin. With a yelp, he unleashed a blast of searing light that blasted the Changeling back into the thickening crowd. The others recoiled with horror as their comrade made collision. Murmurs of shock rippled, as each beheld the amulet.

Recognition dawned on the elders' faces. They leaned in to one another for a fierce discussion in their own tongue.

Andy watched on. His nerves melted away as the Changelings' expressions turned to that of fear. Though it pained him to take advantage of the situation, he knew it was much better than the alternative.

"Listen to me," Andy's voice echoed above the chattering bells. "I know what this looks like, and that I'm uh…kind of a *moron*. But uh, I swear to y'all, I ain't here to bring harm. I'm just trying to save my friends. I really mean the best, I just don't got the best ways of gettin' to it."

The Changelings squinted, looking at each other and back to the boy. Andy let out a sigh.

"And, I'll be honest, y'all ain't livin' in the best of conditions. I can change that. I can bring y'all someplace where y'all won't have to worry 'bout food, or water, or raiders. There's hope up where I'm from, a chance at a new beginnin'. I know y'all got no reason to trust me, but I'm askin' y'all, just…just give me one more chance?"

Slowly, the others turned to Dink.

"This was your plan all along?" one of them rasped. "This is your 'savior from above?'"

Dink shrugged sheepishly. Andy gawked.

"Jeez, what did you tell them?" he asked.

"I might have said something about you being the 'chosen one' leading our people to the 'promised land.'" Dink said.

"You didn't think to tell them *how? Tell me* how?"

"You got me. I did not know this was where we were heading."

The Changelings stared, then turned to each other, discussing amongst themselves. After what felt like ages, the eldest stepped forward. She fixed her gaze on Andy.

"Surface one, your actions have brought great pain to our people. Our sanctuary has been repeatedly uprooted by the very power you now wield. Unfortunately, it appears we have no other choice than to trust you for the time being. Friend Dink has spoken of your character. He believes in your promises of a better life and a new beginning for our kind. We have dwelled in these forsaken lands for far too long. Perhaps it is time for us to seek this new path."

She paused, gauging the reaction of her peers. A nod followed. "We will grant you this chance, surface one. Lead us to this promised land you speak of. But know this—our trust is not given lightly. Should you betray us again, the consequences will be severe."

Andy quivered just a bit, his lips halfway between a grin and a grimace. Honestly he hadn't expected things to work out this well, but who was he to complain?

"Thank you," he said, voice trembling. "I'll uh…I'll do whatever I can to make sure you all get up there, safe an' sound."

Dink laughed nervously and clapped Andy on the shoulder, turning him back around to face the illusory veil.

Just up ahead was the ancient metropolis.

"I am delighted we have reached an understanding." Dink said. "Now can you *please* make sure we do not crash?"

CHAPTER 15

It was a force like a wrecking ball.

The titan burst through the ancient city as easily as tissue paper. Many spires crumbled and shattered, interconnecting beams twisting and snapping. The behemoth continued, unstoppable. Its many passengers were rocked about inside.

Andy gave Drew a sheepish look. Cici certainly wouldn't be happy to learn about the destruction of her ancestral home. He wondered how much that would translate to her older brother figure. Of course, Drew probably had much bigger things to worry about right now—like surviving this trip.

Just above, the undulating mass of the hive caught Andy's eyes. Its surface swam with countless kloons. They seemed blissfully unaware of the encroaching colossus.

Steady, Andy directed the beast to take the hive in its massive maw.

Gently, he commanded.

Slightly veering off-course, the titan carefully grasped the hive in its jaws. The mass squashed and squelched, but remained in one piece. Kloons skittered, honking in alarm and tumbling from their nests.

Andy was acutely aware of the precious cargo within the hive. The slightest miscalculation could spell their doom. Sweat beaded on his brow, all his concentration poured into guiding the titan.

Dust billowed, clouds filled the air, obscuring the beast's vision. Destruction echoed throughout the cavern. It was symphonic, musical almost.

The boy did his best to remain resolute. This was their one chance at escape, after all. He didn't know how long he would have control over this thing.

He called out in his mind.

"I need directions. Where are we going?"

"You know what I require," said the heirloom.

Andy grit his teeth. Another flash in his mind, the vaguely familiar trail to Tanya's treehouse.

"Take it." he said.

And like that, it was gone—sucked away like everything else, replaced with a new vision. A path forward.

Behind the boy, the Changelings chattered in idle conversation. They seemed to be watching every last one of Andy's moves.

Something else entered through the skull flap. A singular kloon, fat and clumsy, managed to wriggle through the narrow opening created by the prior clobbering. One Changeling noticed, then another, and then—before long, the kloon was devoured by a rather gluttonous horde.

Soon after one kloon emerged, another, then another, and another. The trickle turned into a flood as dozens of kloons poured through the flap, honking with angry vigor.

The Changelings licked their lips.

It was kloon carnage, an all-out war ensuing not long after their arrival. They tried their best to peck, gnaw and feed upon the Changelings—only to be lapped up and swallowed whole.

Andy ignored the sounds of gnashing teeth and rubbery crunches. Who was he to deny them their delicacies? They'd all been through so much already. This was more or less their reward for not ripping Andy to shreds.

The voice's directions led him through one passage after another, each one more claustrophobic than the last. The titan hardly fit, its stony sides sparking against the cavern walls. It wasn't surprising, then, when their nice and open pathway came to an abrupt stop.

A dead end wall of stone greeted everyone from the illusory veil. They were going to have to brute force this.

Dig, Andy commanded.

Consider his work done. The boy leaned back. He was drained, one memory after another stolen in quick succession. The scraping of the giant's claws against stone accompanied Andy's idle thoughts.

His mind drifted, trying to sort through the memories he still had. If he couldn't even remember what he had forgotten, how could he possibly know how much had been taken? How much of himself had he sacrificed to this artifact?

Soft footsteps drew Andy from his stupor—Dink's, as he approached the boy's side and sat down.

"Why so glum, friend?" Dink asked. "We are reaching the surface, are we not?"

Andy sighed and pinched his nose. "I'm not so sure if it's gonna be worth it."

"How come?"

"This thing just keeps taking, and taking, but for what? What's the endgame here? What's savin' folks even worth?"

"If you ask me, I would not even bother messing with it further," Dink gestured with his hand. "Ask yourself, why do you feel the need to save others?"

The boy's nose wriggled now.

"I made a promise to someone, and…I don't much like breakin' promises."

"What was the promise?"

"Elena—I promised her grandpa I'd take good care of her. And then, you know, right after making that promise," Andy dramatically flew his thumb through the air into a downward motion. He blew raspberries to emphasize the point.

"Right. Yes. That is a difficult feeling." Dink said.

Andy let out a humorless laugh. "Yeah, well, I thought I could handle it. I thought I was doin' the right thing, but now, I ain't so sure."

Stepping out from the shadows, Drew took a seat next to them.

"Everybody makes promises they can't keep. You took on a pretty heavy burden there, trying to protect a little kid. That's admirable. But you gotta remember, you're a kid, too."

"I guess, but, it just…it *blows*. Feeling like everyone's countin' on you, like you're the only chance people got."

"Let us not blow ourselves out of proportion, friend." Dink said.

Andy cocked his head. "Huh?"

"I would not have so little faith in others. People can pull off incredible things if you give them the chance. Observe what you did for me. You could have let me drown after I tried to kill you, but you saved my life, and you offered my people a chance on the surface. I am sure your friends, wherever they are, they are fighting just as hard to help you keep your promise. I say, if it is out of your control, try not to worry about it so much."

"Worry is all I can do."

"Give yourself grace. You are doing the best you can. That is all anyone can ask for. If you stumble, that is okay. What matters is you keep trying, and that you have others to lean on."

"Yeah. I s'pose. I uh…s'pose I'm just scared, you know?"

"Of failure?"

"Yeah."

"Do not be. There is no point in being scared of something inevitable."

"I don't mean to be a broken record or nothin', but it does seem easier said than done."

Dink leaned back, his eyes growing distant. He thought to himself, then spoke back up.

"I have broken a promise. I failed to protect my friends."

"How so?"

"We went out into the wastes one night, a scavenging trip. Things were getting pretty scarce at home, so we felt we may find something useful among the ruins," Dink brought his knees to his chest.

"We came across this abandoned apothecary—*perfect*—it was stocked with a ton of medicine. Enough supply to last our people for years. We hit the motherlode."

Dink's tone shifted, the levity gone.

"I was so excited, I was not paying attention. I just stuffed my pack full of anything I could grab. I did not hear the stranger sneaking up on us. It happened so fast. One moment, my friend was right there with me. We were...*laughing*. But in the next, he was on the ground. Bleeding out. The bastard slit his throat."

Dink threw his hands up, defeated. A few odd tears streaked down his cheeks.

"I could not do anything, beyond...*running*. I left him there. I was supposed to watch his back, and...and I failed."

Andy knew all too well what the poor guy was going through. And now? All he could think of was if little Elena survived the encounter.

He supposed they would have to wait until they got a chance to crack open the hive to find out.

"I'm sorry, Dink. That must've been awful." Andy said.

Dink wiped his eyes with the back of his hand. "It was. It still is. Some days. But, I mean, life continues. I have to live with it, somehow."

Drew rested his chin on his hand. "I messed up pretty bad, too. When I was younger, closer to your age, I tried to stand up against The Natural Order. I brought a group of close friends to their doorstep, I tried to fight them. I thought they'd just be a bunch of nerds playing dress-up. How freakin' scary could a group of *medieval knights* be? I underestimated them."

Right. The 'revolution' that ended in disaster—Vick told Andy all about it. Drew's little uprising had cost dozens of Supernaturals their lives.

Andy wondered for a moment in just how many ways he paralleled the man sitting beside him. They were both, in a way, responsible for the suffering of their own people.

"I thought I would be *helping* people." Drew said. "But I didn't know what I was doing. None of us did. If we did, I doubt we would have bothered."

Dink nodded. "But we have to keep moving forward, even if it feels like the sands are sucking us down. That is what you need to do. You cannot let broken promises get you down. They are just words. Your actions always speak louder, yes?"

"Yeah. Well. I dunno. What do my actions say about me?" Andy asked.

"I think they say you are kind. Brave. Maybe a little bit dumb."

Andy rolled his eyes. *"Okay."*

"Hey, look where being dumb got us!"

"A little stupidity can go a long way," Drew added.

"Right. Now, keep your chin up and your eyes forward."

"Yup. Thanks, fellas." Andy said.

He looked on ahead, cracks of light that beginning to show through the stone. They were nearly there.

CHAPTER 16

Mr. Hudson was enjoying a nice cup of joe Wednesday morning; after all, why shouldn't he? He's been up for days on end, trying to figure out this unprecedented disaster.

Half of his city's population, gone in an instant! Not even his loyal Rangers could turn up anything concrete.

Sighing, Hudson turned toward the stained glass window behind his desk. The sun was just beginning to rise over the mountains. Had he gotten even a wink of sleep?

The sound of something knocking rattled the room—his office door, it must be.

"Come in," Hudson said. The knocking only intensified, accompanied by the clinking of glass and the rattling of wooden frames.

Hudson scowled, coffee rippling in his designer mug. It rattled and waved until it all began to pour out in hot, messy globs. The tremors were only growing stronger by the minute.

Books tumbled from their shelves, the chandelier swayed precariously. The mayor gripped the edge of the desk. With an involuntarily trembling hand, he reached for the phone and dialed Snoozie's extension.

The line rang once, twice before a sharp crackle filled his ear.

"Snoozan? Are you there? What is going—?"

He was assaulted with a blast of dead air. Hudson cussed and slammed the phone back into its cradle.

Instinctively, his tail coiled around one of the desk legs, seeking stability amidst the turbulence.

Something like a sonic boom sounded. The once-gorgeous window was shattered, reduced to a pile of jagged, multi-colored glass. A gust of wind rushed inside. Hudson shielded his face from the debris.

The shaking reached its crescendo, as the colossus burst through the earth in the distance, flinging soil every which-way.

When the dust settled, Hudson found himself staring at quite possibly the largest creature he had ever seen.

...

The creature's face fell into the surrounding mountains, shaking free the roosting bolters and snow from the trees. Just as soon as it had made its grand entrance did it seem to run out of juice. Dormant, once more.

Deep within the skull of the creature, Andy and Drew led their band of Changelings through the fleshy tunnels and down the nasopharynx—out into the open of its gaping mouth.

The beast made little indication that it was still among the living. Andy had to wonder if it had even been alive to begin with, or if he had been puppeting a massive corpse.

Approaching the pincered hive, Andy raised his voice.

"Listen up, folks! I'm gonna need y'all's help with somethin'. If you're up for helpin', that is. If not, I say you go on and get outta here before things get ugly," he pointed at the city at the center of the valley. "That's your safety net. If you're scared, then go."

A few Changelings looked to each other and back to Andy.

"What is it you ask of us?" one of them asked.

"Up ahead is a kloon hive. A lot of good people are trapped inside of it. A lot of bad people, too. We need to rescue the good people before the bad people can stop us."

A veritable feast of 'kloons,' was it? *My, how exciting.* The Changelings spoke amongst themselves.

"How do we tell the good from the bad?" another asked.

"Bad ones are wearin' armor." Andy said.

"Aye. Easy enough."

A good chunk of them seemed to be on board with the plan. Andy was thankful to have some faith in him, even if he thought it wasn't entirely deserved.

Either way, Hudson had better give these folks a good deal.

The approach toward the hive felt tense. It wasn't lost on a soul, not even Dink as he trotted along behind Andy. Some held on tight to their energy rifles. A few took on alien forms, creatures never quite seen by the surface world. Fewer still could wield shiny-looking spells.

Perhaps they weren't trained in traditional combat, but living in the harsh wastes must have done something for their warrior instinct.

The hive was just up ahead. One lump in the mix had already begun its twitching.

Ksh. Ksh.

KOOSH!

"Henk henk henk henk!"

Dozens of kloons burst from the lump, sprinting at the Changeling army. The grey soldiers did much of the same, voracious, licking their lips. *Blades, blasters, fireballs, oh my!* It was a slurry of slaughter, the kloons meeting their match in the Fae.

Andy managed a few licks as well, batting swaths of kloons into the ground and stomping them to pulps. He mostly kept his energy reserved, though, searching for his friends within every unfamiliar pustule. Something told him he might want to save his strength for later.

Dozens of Changelings stood victorious amidst piles of sugary corpses. Now within the hive itself, the fighting continued, if not very brief. It seemed much of the work inside had already been done.

A few of the inner cocoons had been broken, popped under the pressure of the titan's maw. Some disoriented townsfolk were walking about, already assisting others. Others were already joining in on the fight.

Andy and Drew set to work, using their claws to cut open the remaining sacs and freeing the sleep-deprived figures within. Citizens blinked away the outside light as though they were newborn fawns.

Sure enough, Andy soon happened across his friends, all lumped in within close proximity of each other. Vick, Cici, Tanya, Elena—he breathed a sigh of huge relief when all were accounted for. All except one…Martin. Where was Martin?

He'd have to circle back to the thought, unfortunately. Time was of the essence.

Andy ran to Vick's cocoon first, slashing it open. Vick fell out face-first, coughing and wiping the goo from his mouth. His sputtering only intensified once he realized who his rescuer was. The pair tightly embraced.

"*Andy?*" Vick said. "Gods, you're *alive?!*"

"Mhm," said Andy. "And feelin' right as rain. You wanna give me a hand?"

Vick sniffled, forcing a sneer. "Not really. But I guess I owe you one."

"Two, actually."

Drew approached the pustule where Cici was suspended. After cutting through her prison, she immediately enveloped him in a hug.

"Oh," Drew cleared his throat, patting her on the back. "Missed you too."

"Please don't ever do something crazy like that again!" Cici said.

"I'll…try not to?"

Tanya's cocoon proved a bit more challenging, but not impossible—Vick came in clutch with his 'plasma cutter' spell. Once she was freed, she gave little more than a thankful nod before going to help the other citizens.

Elena came out next. Andy caught her before she could double over.

"Andy," she coughed. "How did you...?"

"I had help. Friends in low places," Andy joked before his face turned deadly serious. "And I promised you—I'm gonna keep you safe."

Their reunion was short-lived, a screech piercing their eardrums. One of the Changelings stumbled into view from an adjacent chamber, a gleaming blade protruding from their chest. The Changeling collapsed after taking a few more helpless steps.

The one responsible emerged next, tearing the blade from the Changeling's back. His focus shifted toward the group, a knight in shining armor.

Then came another, and another, and another, until soon, a whole platoon of Natural Order goons stood with their weapons at the ready.

Without hesitation, their boots thundered against the wet floor. Blades clashed with claws, claws clashed with bone. Sparks flew, a blustering gale of death sweeping through the hive.

Andy and Elena hid within the divot of one busted cocoon. Andy himself didn't intend on hiding forever, but he did need to buy himself some time.

For every knight that fell, two more took their place. They poured out from the adjacent chambers like a Human flood.

Vick's arcane fire scorched their armor. Tanya's vines ensnared and crushed. Cici...well, she wasn't doing much fighting, but her moral support was always appreciated.

"Yeah," she called, pumping her fists up and down. "Get 'em!"

The townsfolk were getting in on the action, too, fighting side by side with the Changelings. A silent understanding had already been reached between the two parties.

Yet even with all their garnered support, the Supernaturals were being overwhelmed, by weaponry, by strategy, by basic Human stubbornness.

Try as he might, Andy was unable to change in his current state. He was exhausted, mentally spent. Even after a long night's rest and a good meal prior, he wasn't sure if he had the focus right now to do it.

The weight of the amulet was still there—his fingertips still idly graced its bronze. There it was again, that powerful temptation. He could turn the tides in an instant. A cruel twist of fate was available, should he wish. Turn the kloons against their former masters…

"Now, child. Use me now. Destroy them."

An image flashed through Andy's mind—Martin, smiling down at him through his beard. Andy just caught a trout. Another bargaining chip.

"No," he said.

"I've made my bargain. Choose."

The voice grew louder, repetitive, insistent—Andy tossed it away in fear. It skid across the floor. Silence. There was a hollowness that fell over him, the absence of this power he'd grown so accustomed to. Nevertheless, his mind was his own again. But the relief was not to last.

His rotten smile was the first thing Andy saw.

From the shadows stepped Lord Vulgo, in all his mottled glory.

"Well done, mutt. You've finally done something reasonable for a change." Vulgo said. His gauntleted hand closed around the amulet. His eyes rolled upward, a moan escaping his lips. Before Andy could do much to protest, he was shot with a cosmic blast.

The impact scorched his chest. Andy's body slamming against the slimy wall. He slid to the floor, coughing.

Vulgo strode forward, amulet pulsing in his hand. It cast an eerie shadow across his pocked face. His teeth were bared in triumph.

"Poor boy. Poor lost, little boy. The sad little boy who couldn't save his friends, even after *all that*. All of that power, and you just threw it right away? You're pathetic, boy. Pathetic."

The knight raised his free hand, otherworldly light coalescing around his fingers. Andy could feel the hairs on the back of his neck stand on end.

"But me? I'm not burdened by such weakness. I'm not an awfully sentimental guy. Even if there was a life for me outside of this one, what good is it now? I'm havin' the most fun when I'm out here, killin' all yous."

Vulgo sent out a pulse of energy that pervaded the hive. From every crevice and corner, dozens more kloons poured forth. They shambled toward him in uniform lines.

The lord stepped toward Andy, and drove his foot right into his ribs.

"Consider this next part my thanks—thanks for giving me the keys to victory."

He kicked Andy again, this time in the face.

"I'm gonna make *sure* you're dead this time before I throw you back into that pit."

Kick. Kick. Kick. The kicks kept on coming, and they didn't seem to be stopping any time soon.

"I almost feel bad for you," Vulgo taunted. "All that potential wasted on someone so...soft." he punctuated the word with another kick to Andy's side. "Did you really think you had what it took? That you could play hero?"

Blood trickled from the corner of Andy's mouth. He could hardly speak.

"You're just a scared little rat, doing what it can to survive. There are no heroes, boy. Only survivors," Vulgo raised his fist, the amulet charging a deathly blow. "And you won't be one of them."

A frosty blast struck Vulgo's hand, encasing both the amulet and his gauntlet in a thick layer of ice.

"Hey, you big dork," Vick's voice called out. "Maybe before you start monologuing, you should make sure the good guy doesn't have backup."

"Come down here, you little bloodsucker, and I'll rip your heart out."

"Strong words from a little man!"

Vulgo scoffed, raising the amulet. A beam of cosmic power shot toward Vick.

The Vampire dodged nimbly. Behind him, one of the lumps was microwaved to a crisp. *He really hoped nobody nice was in there.*

"Wanna try that again?" Vick asked. A bead of sweat dripped down his cheek.

Vulgo sneered, turning back toward Andy. He wasn't about to let this miserable brat distract him.

But Andy was no longer there.

Something else moved in his peripherals. Vulgo snarled, just about to catch it, when his legs were pulled from beneath him. His wrists were ensnared in thick vines, his neck being wrapped as well. Tanya stood over his body, snapping a finger to flourish. The vines subsequently tightened.

As she reached for the amulet, however, Vulgo's fist shot forward, burning straight through the vines and smashing her in the face. Tanya went barreling backward, crashing into a cluster of slimy cocoons.

A wide smile, a constant giggle, the vulgar lord was *clearly* enjoying himself. Vulgo marched toward the downed Tanya.

Vick intervened once more, blasting the floor with a wave of chill. Vulgo slipped, flipped, and landed on his back.

It seemed they had the upper hand, but again, Vulgo raised the amulet into the air. The kloons swarmed Tanya, a wave of them stampeded toward Vick. Several jumped from the walls and ceiling in an attempt to latch on to him. Vick gagged, a few landing on his arm.

"Get it off, get it off!"

While distracted, he got dogpiled by the creatures from above. Vick plummeted to the ground. Vulgo sneered.

"Tear them to *pieces*, my lovelies."

From behind, three arms wrapped around Vulgo like a vice. Cici landed with a thud on his back, one hand grasping for the amulet.

Another figure emerged from the shadows—Drew, throwing a big right hand at Vulgo's helmeted head. The punch connected with a resounding clang, sending the headpiece spinning. Vulgo staggered, momentarily stunned by the force of the blow.

Drew shook his fist out. "Yeah? How's that feel, you big bastard?!"

No response. Vulgo simply reached back, grabbing Cici by the neck and throwing her over his shoulder. Drew, catching his ragdolled friend, let out a rageful cry before Vulgo pummeled him.

Bam! Bam! BAM!

It only took three well-placed strikes. Drew was pretty much done for, falling completely limp to the floor. His fingers continued to scratch at the fleshy ground in silent protest.

Cici got to her feet. Seeing Drew downed, she felt like she had no other choice—she charged Vulgo one last time before she, too, was punted across the hive. The lord laughed. He threw his arms out to his sides.

"This is it, huh? This is *all* the fight you can put up? You poor things. I can see why Talia had such a bleedin' heart for yous. She made you all sound so *fearsome*. So *broken*. If I'd known it would be *this* easy, I wouldn't have bothered with the kloons."

"Hey!"

Another voice cut above—Andy's. Vulgo spun on his heel, and there was the boy, standing tall and proud, and…*with three eyes.*

There was an attempt, at least.

"Changeling," Vulgo laughed. "What are you going to do? More bad impressions?"

"Something like that," said 'Andy.'

The air around 'Andy' shimmered and shifted, like heat waves rising from a sun-scorched road. In seconds, he took on the form of the boy's alter-ego. 'Rex' launched himself at Vulgo, a fuzzy missile inbound. The impact was thunderous, Vulgo sent far off his feet. His armored body crashed through several pustules, showering everyone in viscous sugar water.

Before Vulgo could regain his footing, 'Rex' was on him again, gripping the man by his throat and hoisting him into the air. Despite gagging, Vulgo started to laugh. Before 'Rex' could toss him away like a sack of potatoes, the knight called upon the power of the heirloom. A blinding light erupted from Vulgo's palm, and he clamped down on the choking arm. In an instant, the limb was crystallized.

Cracks spread rapidly from Dink's fingertips to his shoulder. Then, all at once, his arm shattered from Vulgo's weight.

Dink screeched as his form reverted back to normal—Vulgo answered him with a knee to the face. Glistening blood spewed from the Changeling's nose, and he folded to the ground.

An aura of confidence filled the lord—though all around him, things weren't looking good for the rest of his party. The townsfolk had managed to fend for themselves pretty well. The knights were fighting to a standstill. Kloons had been meticulously picked from Vick and Tanya. Drew and Cici were getting back to their feet.

Before long, even with the power of the heirloom, Vulgo could be overwhelmed. Though he hated to admit any sort of inferiority, the knight desperately bargained with the voice for one last surge of power. His 'humanity' didn't matter to him. It never did.

Energy pulsated throughout the man's body, through his armor. It began to smoke, Vulgo broke out into a sweat, then began to scream.

The armor glowed white hot. It seared his flesh, grafted itself onto his skin. *This was it.* This was the feeling he so desperately craved.

Vulgo groaned, a large wave of energy erupting from his body. Most of the townsfolk stepped back, paralyzed, before ultimately scattering. After all, how could they possibly know what he was capable of, now?

Tanya was the first to strike, ensnaring the knight's legs with her vines. She leapt forward and dished out a ten-piece combo of punches and kicks before he swatted her away like a fly.

Vick was next up, hurling a barrage of icicles. They shattered harmlessly against Vulgo's super-armor—he quickly shot Vick down with a cosmic blast.

Andy and Drew took a moment to hide behind a wall.

"Bastard's too strong with that amulet." Drew said.

"Agreed," Andy wiped some blood from his brow. "How do you reckon we get it back?"

Drew's eyes trailed to the head of Meat-Man, still alive and still firmly tied to his belt loop.

"I've got an idea, if we can bait him."

"What's that?"

The man shuddered. "I've seen these guys gnaw through solid steel. Almost lost my hand trying to get one to bite off my cuff."

Andy cringed.

"Do you have any better ideas?" asked Drew.

"No," Andy admitted. "But I'm allowed to be grossed out."

"You're allowed. *Later.*"

Drew looked over the wall to see Vulgo still stomping everyone in combat. They were still kicking, though. Just barely.

"Think you can shift?" Drew asked.

"Maybe for a short bit." Andy said. "I'll try."

"Alright. I'll get things started, then you come in with the big guns."

Andy gulped. "Yup."

"*Hey*. I'm counting on you."

Drew didn't give him time to think it over, charging out from behind the wall. The knight turned, leering.

"Back for more?" Vulgo asked. He raised the amulet.

Drew was ready this time, launching into a slide across the floor, ducking just beneath the ensuing wave of energy. He slid across slime, springing up to latch onto Vulgo's arm. Meat-Man's teeth were bared and ready.

Vulgo readied his other fist. "What the—"

Just then, Meat-Man's razors sunk deep into his armored flesh. The creature gnawed frantically, working overtime, as if he was a beaver in need of a new home. Blood began to spurt. Vulgo slammed Drew against a nearby wall.

The knight's expression teetered on amusement once he realized what was happening. They were really trying something so simple? Against a superior being like him? It was laughable; so laughable, he *laughed!*

"You think I need that useless trinket," Vulgo gripped Meat-Man's lower jaw, pulling. "I am more than what it could possibly do for me," Meat-Man's jaw began to split. Vulgo howled with laughter. "I am his *champion!*"

Shrrrip!

Poor Meat-Man was further mutilated, his wide-eyed cap being tossed to the ground. Vulgo turned to Drew and raised his bloody fist, preparing a crushing blow.

A ginger blur rushed past. The lord was gone.

Drew blinked, following his ears toward a new source of sound—Vulgo getting pounded on by Rex.

Punch after punch dented the helmet, Vulgo spitting out a few rotten teeth. The knight kicked Rex in the gut, rolling back and away from him.

"Why can't you stay dead?" Vulgo growled.

"Dunno." Rex replied. "Why can't you kill me?"

Rex ducked Vulgo's hook, countering with an uppercut. Each whiffed attack only drove Vulgo to further frustration, each movement more erratic, more desperate.

"Aw, what's this?" Rex laughed. "Losin' your nerve already?!"

"Keep talkin' while you can," Vulgo snarled. "I'll cut out your slobberin' tongue the moment I get my hands on you."

"I'd like to see you try, big man." Rex said.

Vulgo threw a fist—another one ducked. Rex tackled him onto the ground, placing his knees on each of Vulgo's arms.

"Nnf! Get off!"

Rex leaned in with a wide grin, dog-breath wafting into Vulgo's face.

"Make me."

Seizing the opening, Drew picked up a dropped sword from the ground. Its silver handle burned through the flesh of his palms, but he kept hold, walking it over to the downed lord. He brought it down, again, and again. Vulgo screeched, thrashing, rolling from side to side, doing anything to get the weight off his arms.

One last time, the sword fell. Blood sprayed the three of them.

The knight's hand was severed. Drew swiped it off the floor, tearing the amulet away from its clutches.

That's when the voice began to speak his name.

CHAPTER 17

Ice massaged his brain, the low hum growing louder; Drew's world had gone still in that instant, his surroundings quiet. Just him, in a black void, listening to the voice.

"Hello."

"Who's there?"

"An ally."

Drew brought the heirloom to his face. Was it speaking to him?

"I've been waiting a long time for someone like you." it purred. "I can feel your strength, your potential…your pain."

Flashes of skewered bodies, Supernaturals dead by the dozens. A failed coup, gone wrong in every way. Drew tried to force the memory out of his head, but it stuck, haunting him, decaying his conscience. The screams echoed, the smoke filling his lungs.

"So many lost. You think their blood is on your hands, as you think of hers."

Another vision—that of his mother, lying close, twitching on the forest floor. A crossbow bolt stuck out from her back.

Drew was pinned underneath, the same bolt piercing his lungs. He tried to tell her he loved her, that it was going to be alright, but he couldn't make a sound.

Blood seeped from the edges of her lips. Carol drew her last breath.

He was just trying to make things right. And he had led them all right here—right to *her*.

"You weren't strong enough. You weren't fast enough. You weren't *enough*."

Drew's grip tightened. The voice continued, words both like balm and a blade.

"It does not have to be that way. I can give you the power you crave. The power to protect each and every last one of them. No more sorrow, no more pain."

The dark veil lifted.

Vulgo gripped Rex's throat with his remaining hand, threatening to crush his windpipe. The Werewolf's form quickly deteriorated into that of Andy's. It seemed he was all out of juice.

All around the battlefield were littered the battered bodies of his friends. Kids, for sure, but the only real companionship he seemed to have. They all fought tooth and nail to get this heirloom away from Vulgo—its word must be worth something.

The voice continued.

"Become my champion, and I swear that no harm shall come upon those you love."

The man scoffed at the idea. *Him, in service?*

"What do you want from me?" Drew asked.

"I want you to destroy The Natural Order."

"What? Haven't you been helping them?"

The entity paused. "This form, unfortunately, demands a sort of subjugation in order to flourish. To put it lightly, I've had to allow for fate to take its course. Do not mistake my aid for endorsement. It is merely the accumulation of knowledge, which, in due time, will be used to punish those responsible for your suffering. You will be my instrument—their tormentor."

Tormentor? It was very tempting. Drew hadn't much trouble thinking about it. All the people he's failed, all the friends he's lost, his family, taken. What little power he had was forcibly revoked for having *dared* challenge the status quo. He glared at the cuff around his wrist.

"What's it cost? A memory?"

"A spare few precious ones, to save their lives. What is it worth to you, Drew Warren?"

He looked at Andy, dangling helplessly by Vulgo's hand.

The power to prevent loss. The power to save them.

That's all he ever needed.

"Are you ready to become the hero?"

"I am."

As the words formed, a surge of power coursed through his veins, igniting every nerve. It was like liquid fire racing through his bloodstream. Arcane runes blossomed on his skin like flowers, covering his body. They shone with a magenta light which pulsed in time with Drew's heartbeat.

Vulgo was near-blinded by the light, releasing the kid in his clutches. Clearly this was something that demanded his attention. He blocked out the cosmic rays with his hand as best he could.

Andy scrambled backward, taking in Drew's new and 'improved' look. He wondered what he must have sacrificed to get it.

Hopefully not anything too important.

The light dimmed. Vulgo lowered his arm. His lip curled, not so much worried as he was annoyed.

"You know, you lot are really starting to piss me off," he said.

"Feeling's mutual." Drew replied.

"*Mutual?* You're the ones who came here uninvited, muckin' up our world with your filth."

"We're just trying to live our lives, same as anyone else. Sorry you're so scared of that."

Vulgo laughed. "I'm not scared of you magic-wieldin' yobs. I *loathe* you. All this potential you waste, all what should've been *ours.*"

"Don't tell me you're jealous."

186

"Of course I'm jealous. The rest of us have to live out dull lives, work dull jobs, break our backs for hours on end, all for *the man*, all with the knowledge that we're rotting with every second. Human potential has never been so limited."

The man's teeth ground together, flakes of enamel mixing with his spittle.

"Meanwhile, *you* lot get to live your fantasy lives in fairy-tale land, where magic solves all your problems and you can live to be a thousand. All because *your God* decided to skip us over."

Drew squinted. "What are you talking about?"

"We're all a bunch of failed experiments, you and I—play things for whoever lives *in there*," Vulgo pointed a gnarled finger at the heirloom. "*He* made us first, and he tossed us to the wind. All for this cheap gimmick, for humanity: version two-point-o."

A beat of pause was given. Drew looked down at the heirloom in his hand.

"Yeah? I guess that means he found the next best thing."

Vulgo's eye twitched. He cracked his knuckles.

"Prove it," he snarled.

The two stared each other down for a beat. The ground trembled.

WHOOSH!

A resounding leap toward one other—their collision was like that of two freight trains, sending shockwaves through the hive. Drew's fist, crackling with energy, smashed into Vulgo's garbled visage. The force of the blow sent him careening through three layers of wall, leaving man-shaped holes in his wake.

Vulgo rose, rubble falling from his person. The man was just getting started. He picked a sword up from off the ground, wiping his thumb across the blood-stained blade.

Drew ran right at him, charging another blow.

Baring a wicked smile, Vulgo flung the sword, its hilt smashing Drew in the shin and knocking him off his feet. Like a boulder falling from a mountain, Vulgo dove, threatening to crush Drew.

Drew rolled to the side just in time.

KA-RUCK!

The ground cracked beneath the impact.

There was the sword lying next to him; Drew grabbed it and swung it at Vulgo once again. The knight blocked each strike with his gauntlets, sparks burning through the air. On its next subsequent swing, Vulgo tore the blade from Drew's scalded hands. He smashed the man's face in with a headbutt.

Stars exploded into Drew's vision, the taste of blood thick on his tongue. He spat crimson and grinned.

"Is that all you got, bug boy?" he asked.

Vulgo wouldn't dignify that with a response. He ran at Drew, his sword raised high. Drew ducked underneath the whistling blade and drove his fist into Vulgo's gut. He half-expected his knuckles to be broken from that, but no. The knight doubled over, wheezing. Counting his blessings, Drew followed with an uppercut, one that nearly took Vulgo's head off.

The lord reeled, Drew pressing forward, unleashing a flurry of magic-cushioned blows. Each shot sent a tremor through the hive, the air crackling with electricity. Vulgo's armor dented and cracked, ichor oozing from its fissures.

Vulgo caught Drew in the face with a backhand. Drew's vision swam with floaters. Still, he managed to block the next strike. The two grappled instead, straining against one another with their respective inhuman strength.

Straining, Drew barely managed to wrestle the knight to the ground. He brought down his fist for one devastating punch after another. The ground beneath them cracked, warped and shattered. Both of them went hurtling down the mountainside.

They traded blow after blow as they further spiraled. Each punch let out a thunderclap of sound. An avalanche of rubble began to follow, wiping out everything in its path. Behind the landslide, Andy and his friends came sliding down. *As if they were going to miss this.*

Both combatants bounced and skidded across the ground as they came to the bottom of the hill. They were already getting to their feet by the time the dust cleared. Energy welled in their hands.

Like gunslingers at high noon, they both drew palms, crackling with cosmic might. The blinding beams collided in the air. An explosion of color accompanied.

Blackening skin snaked its way up Drew's arm as the magic took its toll on his body. It was so much power, too much, it was destroying him from the inside out.

One thing he figured was that it must be doing the same to Vulgo.

The lord's expression was obviously pained, his jaw agape and trembling. His head rolled back along his shoulders as he pushed his beam. His gauntlets glowed white hot, to the point that they were melting. He couldn't keep this up for much longer.

Drew pushed harder, his beam progressing further. Flecks of skin on Vulgo's face began to peel away. He screamed, louder and louder, strained harder and harder, but it was of no use. In moments, Vulgo was enveloped in Drew's beam, engulfed in a scorching ray of pure energy.

The lord fell to his knees, then his back. He twitched wildly, foaming at the mouth. His face was burned black, pus oozing from multiple wounds. His armor had warped and bent out of shape.

Drew flexed his scalding fingers as he approached. There was a hatred in his eyes, a raw, unrestricted contempt. Andy knew such hatred once—and he knew no good would come of it. Swallowing hard, he started toward the two warriors.

"It's…not fair," Vulgo weakly moaned. "It isn't…fair at all."

"Life's not fair," Drew said, driving his heel into Vulgo's chest. The lord cried out.

"Hey," Andy warned, tugging Drew's leg. "He's done. We don't need to—"

"To what? Sink to his level? Is that what you're going to say?"

"We don't. It's not too late."

"I don't need a lecture right now, especially not from *you*. This rat bastard's had this comin' for a long time."

"There's no honor in kickin' someone while they're down."

Drew scoffed, pushing Andy to the side. "Oh, shut up. What good is honor? We're already monsters to them."

"We don't have to be monsters."

"Well frankly, I'd rather be a predator than prey. For years, we've done nothing but fear these apes. But we don't have to be afraid of them anymore."

In his palm, the heirloom began to glow with that otherworldly light. Andy felt paralyzed.

"Whatever you're thinkin', it ain't worth losin' your—"

"Can it, kid! *I'm* the hero here!"

The heirloom flashed. A beam of intense light engulfed Vulgo's body.

FWOOSH!

The light faded. For a moment, nothing seemed to have changed. The battlefield remained still. The scent of burning ozone was heavy. Drew still stood tall over the prone lord.

Andy blinked, squinting to see what had happened. Vulgo's chest rose and fell with shallow breaths.

Cici approached, careful of disturbing the loose stones. She cocked her head.

"I don't understand, what did you—"

Her words caught in her throat. Vulgo's skin began to undulate.

They were small tremors at first, like the surface of a pond disturbed by a pebble. Then, the movement intensified, flesh rippling in nauseating waves.

He opened his mouth to scream, but only a strangled gurgle escaped. His body convulsed, armor creaking and groaning as it strained against the transformation.

"What's happening to me?!" he asked.

Vulgo's skin bubbled with a sickening rhythm. His armor split at the seams. Glimpses of lumpy flesh churned underneath. The body desperately tried to maintain some semblance of its original form, but it was futile.

One by one, with a sickening series of pops, Vulgo's body burst apart like an overripe fruit. His howls echoed through the valley, his body tearing itself apart. In his place writhed dozens of newborn kloons, struggling to orient themselves.

Andy stumbled backwards, about to puke. He let it all out onto the cold earth. Cici patted him on the back, though she considered following in his footsteps.

"Tep's sake." Vick said.

"It's what he deserved," Drew growled. "It's what *all* of them deserve."

"Don't reckon anybody deserves *that*." Andy said.

"Whatever," Drew rolled his eyes, pacing back up the mountain.

"Where are you going?" Cici asked.

"To finish what I started. You're all welcome to come with if you want. But don't you dare get in my way again."

The others looked at one other. They *did* need to help liberate more of the hive, this much was true. Andy still hadn't found his father, given the chaos of the situation. Maybe now would be the perfect opportunity.

But Drew didn't wait for a response. He just kept walking up the pass.

Andy had to wonder to himself…

Did they really just save the valley?

...

Townsfolk poured into the streets, the news of the victory spreading like wildfire. Everyone's faces lit up, their cheers erupted, a chorus of whoops and hollers echoed through the city streets. Loved ones embraced one another. All was well. *Mostly.*

Just about everyone found themselves swept away to the old dive for drinks. The atmosphere inside was what you'd expect from one of these places on a Saturday night. Glasses clattering, foam spilling, laughter ringing.

Geb could barely keep with the demand, his tiny hands working overtime on supplying brews and burgers.

A Minotaur belted out tunes, a Grim played along on the drums. The melody was infectious, the floor packed with dancing bodies of all shapes and sizes.

Drew sat at the bar, surrounded by his throng of new admirers. They hung on his every word as he recounted the battle. The heirloom pulsed softly in his pocket.

Andy, Vick, Cici and Tanya hovered on the outskirts of the crowd, exchanging sour glances. They did their best to catch Drew's attention, but he seemed oblivious to their presence.

"Hey," Andy raised his voice above the others. "Can we talk for a sec?"

No response. Drew didn't even turn his head. He continued to pepper his audience with tales of his heroics, his voice growing louder and more animated.

"Drew please," said Cici "We're really worried about you."

Still no response. Drew slammed a shot and pounded the glass on the bar with enough force to make everyone jump.

Vick's eyes narrowed. "Hey, jerk, your friends are trying to talk to you!"

Drew's head turned slightly in their direction.

"Look, kids. Why don't you go home? We won. It's late. Your parents are probably worried about you."

Andy bit his tongue and stepped back, growling under his breath. Tanya followed, then Cici, then lastly Vick, though the Vampire didn't leave without one last sting.

"Be careful when you step outside. Wouldn't want your head flying into the clouds."

The group stepped out into the chilly night, the sounds of revelry fading behind them. Andy kicked a loose pebble, sending it skedaddling across the cobblestone.

"Gods, it's like we don't even exist," Cici said. She hugged herself against the cold.

Vick scoffed. "Probably his fancy new powers. He thinks he's too good for us now that he's the talk of the town."

"I'm not so sure," Andy murmured. "I wouldn't be surprised if the heirloom took away somethin' about us."

"More reason for us to want nothing to do with him." Vick said with a sneer. "He'd give that away for a little taste of power?"

"Come on, Vick. It's not like that," Andy looked down, playing with his hands. "It's...it's like a worm that just gets into your head and keeps taking, and taking. And it's a good talker. Talked me into...into *somethin'.*"

Tanya gave Andy a pat on the arm. She gave a rare and reassuring smile.

"You didn't lose us at least," Cici said. "We appreciate it."

"Totally." Vick said. "So what do we do about *him?*"

"For now I just say we keep an eye out. Not much else to do besides that."

The others nodded, facing down the breezy street. An adventure for another time, perhaps. For now, they all felt it best to follow Drew's advice, to some extent, and return home.

They wondered if they'd be able to get any sleep.

Andy couldn't help but shiver as he said his goodbyes. He could hear the faintest whisper of commotion from the pub, though he tried to shake off that nasty feeling.

Inside, Drew raised another glass in toast, oblivious to the worry of his friends. The voice of the heirloom purred in his mind, drowning out all other thoughts.

"Revel this night, my champion. The first step is complete. Soon, we shall manifest our destinies. We shall change the world, you and I. *Together.*"

Drew's lips curled into a smile as he drained his glass. The real work was just beginning.

CHAPTER 18

City hall was lined with decades of portraits featuring Mr. Hudson.

One would think there would be other mayors over the years—but suppose this fellow forgot to adopt the Human idea of democracy.

Andy paced back and forth in the lobby, glaring at the paintings as they passed him by.

*Waiting, waiting…*how long were they going to make him wait? His hands fidgeted with the strings of his hoodie. Sweat condensed around his forehead. He wasn't sure how much longer he could bear it.

Snoozie's voice cut through the tumult.

"Mr. Hudson is ready to see you now!"

Andy spared no time stepping into the old elevator. The contraption creaked as it ascended, an iron cage on its last legs. Many floors passed Andy's vision before he reached the top.

Ding.

Stepping out onto the top floor, there was the immediate scent of burning tobacco—cherry flavored. Andy took a few steps across the hardwood floor before a flood of relief washed over him. His eyes locked onto the familiar figure sitting in one of Hudson's chairs; Martin, alive and well.

Not a moment to lose. Andy leapt right into his father's arms, hugging him tight.

"Where have you been?!" Andy demanded. "I've been worried sick!"

"I was helpin' evacuate folk—didn't even stop to think it was you that…" Martin choked up. "By God, it was *you*. I thought I lost you."

"I know. I'm sorry."

"Don't be sorry, boy! You're here. That's all that matters."

Andy sniffled. "Yeah, s'pose you're right."

"Of course I am," Martin laughed and ruffled Andy's hair.

Hudson cleared his throat. *Ah, yes.* They had both completely blocked him out, they were so caught up with each other. The Gorgon sat with his fingers crossed, elbows on his desk. The light glinted off his glasses.

"Oh," Andy said. "Howdy, Mr. Hudson."

"Hello, Mr. Kessler. Please have a seat."

Andy dutifully obeyed, taking a spot at his father's side. His leg nervously jostled up and down.

"Mr. Kessler," Hudson started. "Let me begin by expressing my gratitude for your heroism in defending this here city. You showed bravery and resourcefulness in the face of an unprecedented threat, and in doing so, have saved countless lives."

Ahah. Andy was taken aback. He wasn't quite sure how to respond to the onset of praise.

"I just did what anyone else would've done, sir."

"Perhaps," Hudson conceded. "But the fact remains that you went above and beyond for your friends, and for your city. For the latter, you have my thanks."

During the briefest moment, a smile flashed on Hudson's face.

"However, I think it best we address the manner in which you chose to confront this threat."

Gulp. The boy listened intently.

"Earthquakes of that magnitude don't just happen in West Virginia. You done started a rumor mill the likes of which ain't gonna die down any time soon. Talks of giant monsters, dozens of abducted Humans—you know how much that's gonna shake up the outside world?"

Andy's heart sank. "Sir, I—"

"Luckily, we've got folks hard at work helping to maintain some semblance of secrecy. But with The Order on our tails…"

Oh, man. Andy knew his actions were going to have consequences, he did, but he didn't think for a second of how severe they would be.

"I'm awfully sorry, sir. I didn't mean to cause any trouble."

Hudson waved his hand dismissively. "No apologies needed, Mr. Kessler. What's done is done. I say the ends justify the means. We're just gonna have a lot on our plate when it comes to our future. I say, I think we're about ready for it. Reckon we've been ready for a while."

The mayor sighed. "Now, truth be told, I can't say it won't affect you. I'm afraid that due to current circumstances, it would be unwise for you two to maintain regular contact."

Andy felt a lump rise in his throat. He held his tongue.

"Now, I know, I know. I'm saying this for your own good. The government ain't the only ones monitoring things closely. Any unusual activity, like your correspondence, magic or not, it's gonna start drawing unwanted attention."

Martin nodded slowly, downcast. He turned to Andy, but couldn't quite meet the boy's eyes. It was goodbye, yet again, only somehow it hurt even worse.

"I understand, Mr. Hudson." he said.

"Good," Hudson leaned back in his chair. "This won't be permanent, of course. We'll make arrangements for you folks to get nice and acquainted again soon enough."

There was the bright side, at least. Just how long was the wait going to be?

Hudson cleared his throat. "Andy? What say you, son?"

196

"Yes, sir." Andy said. "That sounds like a plan."

It was settled then. Clapping his hands, Hudson swiveled his chair to gaze outside.

"Say, Kessler-Senior, maybe you'd like to see your boy's living arrangements before you go."

Martin perked up a bit, looking to Andy for confirmation. The boy nodded fast.

"Sure!" he said. "That sounds great!"

Hudson smiled again, raising his pipe to his lips.

"Excellent. I'll arrange for a Ranger transport to escort you from the valley in a few hours. Do feel free to go along your merry way. I trust you'll not bother the locals. I've already got my work cut out for me."

Finally, after a whole year of being separated, finally they'd get to spend some quality time with each other again—and no surveillance to boot!

Andy hurriedly hopped out of his chair and dragged his old man to his feet.

"And Andy," Hudson's voice made Andy pause like a deer in headlights. "Do be careful where you take your father. I'd hate for y'all to have a paparazzi on your tail—Mr. Roldán's company included."

Andy gave a nervous laugh. "Sure thing, Mr. Hudson. We'll probably just go right to my place."

"Good," Hudson bowed his head. "Enjoy your time together, Mr. Kessler."

"Thank you, Mr. Hudson! I will!"

The boy pulled his father along toward the elevator. Martin chuckled, allowing himself to be dragged. He gave Hudson a nod of thanks before the elevator doors slid shut.

"So, this place of yours," Martin started. Andy bounced on his heels.

"Ohh, just wait 'til you see it! It's real nice, old school, got a kitchen and everything."

Ding.

Andy ran straight for the front door once the elevator stopped.

"And where exactly do you think you're going?" another voice asked.

Once more halted in his tracks. Andy spun around, red in the face as he made eye contact with Snoozie. Her multiple arms were crossed.

"Just uh…showin' my dad my home." Andy said. "Mr. Hudson said it was okay."

"Not dressed like that, you aren't."

"I'm sorry?"

Snoozie huffed and ducked underneath her desk, pulling out a large linen bedsheet. Two large holes were poked in it. She handed it over to Martin.

"What am I supposed to do with this?" the old man said.

"Use your imagination," Snoozie winked at Andy.

Martin grudgingly threw the sheet over his head. The makeshift holes gave him just enough visibility to navigate. Andy stifled a laugh.

"Uhuh," Martin grumbled as he made his way out the door. "Yuck it up."

The city streets were busy as usual underneath the afternoon sun. Winged folk flew overhead, a few bolters swam by in the river canals. Martin kept his gaze fixed forward for the most part. He did not want to even attempt to comprehend some of the horrors which made themselves known in the moment.

Andy, desensitized to it all, led the way with a skip in his step. He showed Martin to the library, with its unique aquatic section, then pulled him past the various food stalls that lined the square. Martin wasn't sure he'd ever eat what these creatures considered cuisine, but he had to admit, some of it smelled pretty good.

They made their way down to the lake, the pop-up shops giving way to towering pines. A well-worn path wound through the woods toward a cabin perched on the shore. The potted plants out front looked parched. Andy grabbed a pail for water.

"Make yourself at home," he called to Martin as he ran toward the lake. "I'll be right in."

Martin stepped inside. The cabin was warmly lit, multiple lamps left on, sun flowing in through the beige curtains. He hadn't realized it until he looked at the long, plush chairs, but the old man was exhausted. He took a seat and threw his legs up on one, kicking his boots off onto the floor. A restful sigh escaped his lips.

"You've done good for yourself, son." Martin said.

Wheeze!

He felt something heavy hop onto his diaphram—Otto, having been without company for days, was kneading the old man's chest. Martin felt like he could hardly breathe.

Andy came back inside, laughing when he spotted his dad already making himself at home.

"He seems to like you." Andy said. "Also, I uh, was hopin' to give you a tour."

"I know. Just give me a minute to rest my eyes."

"You ain't fallin' asleep on me, are you?"

"I'm not."

"Good," Andy flopped down on the couch adjacent to Martin's. He stared at the ceiling for a good few moments.

"Pa, can I ask you somethin'?"

"What's up?"

Andy creased his brow. "What is it exactly that we're forgettin'?"

Martin turned, caught off guard by the question. "What do you mean?"

"The heirloom. It took somethin' from us both. What did it take?"

The pale of realization washed over Martin's dark features. "Andy, what did you do?"

"What I...*had* to, in order to save everyone. But, something's missin'. And, the heirloom, it said it took the memory from you, too."

The old man cringed. He thought back to his home, to those unfamiliar photos which lined the walls.

He thought once more about that woman.

"I think she's your mother." he said.

It was like all his limbs had fallen asleep at once. Andy tried to bite the feeling back. It was so uncomfortable, the way it started to fester in his dancing fingers—regret, unimaginable regret. What *did* he do?

"I just wanted to save everyone," the boy repeated, tearing up. Martin watched, letting out a sigh.

"And I wanted to save you," he replied. "That *thing* told me that it's what she would have wanted. While I don't regret it for one second, I…wish the price had been different. It ain't nothin' but a sick joke, you know. They say you have two deaths. The first time you die, and then the next, when you are *completely* forgotten. I'm not sure what happened to your mama, Andy. But sometimes, I think that it's really me who killed her in the end."

Andy felt a pang of guilt, like a migraine beginning to spread toward the neck. He hardly wanted his father to feel the same way.

"Do you think she's happy that we survived?"

"Maybe she is. I doubt it's anything more than bittersweet."

"Well, I don't think that at all."

Silence. There was nothing really more to say on the matter, but such a depressing note to end on. Andy's lips hung open for a few moments longer as he tried to think of something pertinent, but nothing came.

"So what are you gonna do when you get home?" he asked as he wiped his eyes.

"When I get home?" Martin puffed his cheeks. "I'm not sure. I imagine work's gonna be a hassle, if I even still have my job. Elena's not too keen on the idea of school, either."

"How are things with her? I never got a chance to ask."

"They're…complicated. I ain't so sure this arrangement was too good of an idea."

"We didn't really have much of a choice."

"Still. The fact that she has to stay with me, after—"

"It was an *accident.*" Andy cut in.

"It still happened."

Martin shifted his legs to the side and sat up, resting his face in his hands. "I wish I could say it didn't. I wish I had known better."

"You didn't. You do now. It's not healthy to beat yourself up over that stuff."

"The point is that she hates me. And I'm probably the last person that should be taking care of her. She deserves to be happy, not stuck with a murderer."

"Well, she can't stay here, I know that much," Andy patted his stomach a few times. "I'm not sure. That is tough."

"Why can't I stay here?" a tiny voice asked.

Andy and Martin both looked up, jostled.

Elena stood in Andy's bedroom doorway, wrapped in a blanket.

"Mr. Hudson says so." Andy said. "Lettin' a Human stay here would be openin' up a whole can of worms we don't wanna get into."

"Why?"

"I don't know. It's just…the way it is."

"That's *stupid.* I want to stay with you."

"I know you do," Andy sighed. "Look, Elena—can you come sit down with us for a sec?"

The girl hesitantly stepped in place, debating whether or not she wanted to hide away in the bedroom again. She couldn't say no to Andy, though. He just saved her life, among other things.

Scrupulous, Elena entered the living room and took a seat on the chair next to Andy. She kept her eyes on Martin the whole time, lower lip quivering.

Andy looked at Martin expectantly.

"Well? Do you have somethin' you'd like to say?"

The old man swallowed and sat up. Otto meowed in protest.

"Elena, I'm sorry."

Elena pouted, though her focus remained locked. Martin nervously rubbed his hands together.

"I'm sorry for what happened. I'm sorry for what I did to you. You have no reason to ever forgive me."

The little girl crossed her arms. Her gaze finally broke away.

"You killed Daddy," she said, voice shaky.

"I know. And I wish things were different. I wish there was a way you could get your family back. I wish there was a way you'd never have to see me again. But right now, you're torn between two worlds, one where you belong, and one where…you might not so much. You need to make a choice, Elena."

Martin turned toward Andy. His old eyes bore conflict.

"There are ways you can stay here, of course. You could have Andy here bite you."

Andy scowled heavily at the idea. Martin continued.

"It's hypothetical. But I'm saying, if you really wanted, you could reject your Human side for good. But, would it be the best life for you? To never be allowed to leave this valley? I can't damn you to that life in good conscience. It would be a big choice, one I'm not sure you can make on your own just yet," Martin sighed. "It's…hard to say, really."

The old man's gaze fell back to the wooden floor.

"I want you to have the whole world. It's what you deserve, after everything you've been through. I care for you, Elena. I'm sorry things turned out the way they did."

Elena stewed on the old man's words for some time.

"That's what Daddy wanted too." she said.

There was a gossamer thread of understanding established. The pain and anger that had consumed her for so long died down, replaced now by a sense of longing.

"I miss Daddy." she said.

Martin nodded. "I know. If I could go back and change things, I would in a heartbeat."

The girl's bottom lip trembled. "But you can't. Nobody can."

"That's right. But what I can do is try to make things hurt a little less. I want to give you the life your daddy wanted to give you."

Andy watched. He knew full well the pain Elena was feeling. He knew the struggle that it was to forgive someone. He'd been through it with her grandfather, for the revenge he wrought on the Kessler family. He'd seen it consume Drew to the point that he could no longer recognize him.

He knew her struggle, and how much she needed to feel safe again.

"Elena," Andy placed a hand on her shoulder. "I know it's hard to imagine it right now, but I really think givin' Pa a chance could be good for you. I know my Pa, he wouldn't ever hurt a fly if he could help it. What happened that night, if he would've known, I doubt he would've…"

A hard swallow. Andy sighed.

"Listen. He wants to take care of you. An', he took care of me, an' look how I turned out? I'm a pretty alright guy, I think?"

Elena sniffled, considering the words carefully. She looked at Martin, really looked at him, and saw the remorse in his eyes.

Maybe, just maybe she could find it in her heart to make things work.

"I don't want to be mad at you," she said. "But I don't know if I can forgive you, either."

"You don't have to." Martin said. "All I'm askin' for is a second chance."

Elena hesitated, squeezing Andy's hand. She looked up at the boy, then back over to the old man.

"…I think I can do that."

A ray of sunshine streamed in through one of the cabin windows, striking the back of Elena's head. That dang halo came back. Martin's heart could hardly take it. A smile was hidden somewhere beneath that bushy beard of his, mixed in with a tear or two.

Not content to be stewing in his emotion for long, the old man sniffled, wiped his eyes, and stood up, fixing his hat to his head.

"Well, boy, you said you wanted to give me a tour of the place."

Andy raised an eyebrow. "Right now? Okay, I mean, sure."

The boy got to his feet, gesturing for the others to follow.

CHAPTER 19

Cici stood before Drew's door, her eye fixed on a bright red eviction notice. The paper fluttered in the building's stale draft, almost taunting her indecision.

She raised one of her arms, fingers curled, ready to knock. But something stopped her—was it fear? Uncertainty? Or maybe the growing realization that Drew might not even be behind the door?

Whatever it was, it was doing a great job at repelling her from the confrontation. She lowered her arm, defeated, and turned away. Her footsteps made hardly a sound as she sauntered along the stripped-down hall.

Cici pushed past the heavy door and through the Yellow Devil's Dive. The scent of his signature sausages was no longer there, replaced by the smell of wet paint. She exited the building, the bell above tinkling halfheartedly, as if it, too shared her gloom.

Cold air embraced her as she stepped onto the curb. Her friends sat huddled at the park across the street. Andy and Vick talked about something just beneath the sound of the wind.

Andy's ears twitched as Cici approached.

"Any luck?" he asked. Cici shook her head, antennae drooping.

"I couldn't do it," she admitted, her usual bubbly voice falling flat. "The notice is still there. I doubt he's even come home."

"Well, where else could he be?" Vick asked.

"I don't know. But I'm worried. Plus I left my bag at his place."

"We're all worried," Andy said. "Just try an' hold out hope, alright?"

"Alright," Cici said. "I will. I just…I don't know what I'm gonna do now. All my plans for this weekend are ruined."

Andy shrugged. "We could watch that show with ya, if you wanted. The clown one."

"We could?" Vick asked. Andy socked him in the arm. "*D'ow!* Right, yeah. We could."

"We could," Cici repeated. She looked downtrodden again as she remembered, "Oh. I kinda wanted to show Tanya, too. Plus the whole first season's in my bag."

"Where *is* Tanya?" Andy asked.

"Rangers are workin' her overtime, I hear," Cici said. "There's still some folks missing by the sounds of it, and they need someone who knows the caves to navigate."

"Good for her, I guess." Vick said.

"I'm a bit jealous, I'll admit. I really wanted to see more of the city."

"I think you're the only person here that does."

"All the more reason to hire me," Cici turned to Andy. "You heard about Dink yet?"

Andy tapped a finger to his chin. "Maybe we ought to pay him a visit. Meat-Man too."

"Oh, yeah," Vick said as he took out his notepad. "I still need to talk to them."

"Maybe we ought to see how they're feelin' first." Andy said.

Vick huffed. "I guess."

The trio made their way through town, passing by the odd home or two before the clinic came into view. The moment they opened the door, that familiar hospital scent hit their noses. Sterile, as always. Save for a few copies of the local paper, the waiting room sat empty. Vick's smiling mugshot could be spotted on the front page, as well as a few photos of the new excavation site.

Cici approached the front desk. A Grim swaddled in preservative wraps greeted her, empty eyes scanning the group over.

"We're here to see Dink and Meat-Man, please." Cici said.

The Grim glanced up, pointing a bony finger toward the nearby corridor.

"Room 13, down the hall and to the left. Don't cause any trouble."

The teens nodded their heads and hurried along. They could hear the faint beeping of medical devices and the murmur of someone's voice. Cici knocked softly before pushing the door open.

Inside, Dink lay propped up on a bed, looking totally drained. His complexion was paler than before, and his normally vibrant hair had grown dull, stark white. Where his right arm should have been, there was only a bandaged stump.

Despite his condition, Dink still managed a smile as the group entered.

"Ah. Finally come finish the job?"

Andy laughed. "To finish my rounds for the day. How're you feeling?"

"Oh, I am alright," Dink coughed. "Though I imagine my exercises will be more difficult going forward."

Andy's gaze drifted to the bedside table, where a pot of dirt sat. On top, covered by fuzzy spores, was Meat-Man's head. His jaw had properly regenerated, though missing a few teeth, giving him one heck of an overbite. His eyes all focused on different members of the group.

"Gods, is he alive?" Vick asked.

"As alive as he can be," Dink said. "The doctors are not sure what to make of him. But he seems to be hanging in there."

"Bones," the Mycarnid rasped. "Meat-Man needs bones!"

"We'll look for some later, buddy, don't you worry." Cici said.

Andy pulled up a chair and sat by Dink's bed. "I'm glad you two are alright. Bit of a wild ride, huh?"

"That is one way to express that," Dink chuckled, wincing.

Vick leaned in closer, notepad at the ready.

"So, about your home…anything juicy you wanna share? My readers are dying to know more about you guys."

"Perhaps another time. I am still rather loopy." Dink said.

"Right, right." Vick tucked the notepad away, sheepishly exchanging a glance with Andy.

"Have any of the other Changelings come to visit yet?" Andy asked. "How are they adjustin'?"

"The ones who come to visit have told me negotiations are going well. I am afraid without boots on the ground myself, I cannot be so certain. Have you seen them walk among you? My people?"

"A few, from time to time, but not many since we came back up here."

Dink shrugged. "I would say give it a few days. We are bound to get into trouble soon."

"Right."

"How are things with you, friends? Were you able to speak with the red-haired one?"

"Not yet, but I'm not giving up," Cici said, though her earlier actions didn't convince her of such.

"We're just getting ready for the festival," Vick added. "They're holding a rerun of it this weekend."

Dink nodded, head turning back up toward the ceiling.

"Perhaps I will come along, once I feel better."

"You want us to get out of your hair?" Cici asked.

"Mm. I suppose I should be getting rest, if that is to be the case." Dink said.

"We'll let you go, then," said Andy. "But hey, once you're back on your feet, maybe we can throw your folks a 'homecoming' party. You know. For your new home."

"The festival sounds fun," Dink said. "A party does, too."

"*Bones,*" Meat-Man roared. "Bring bones for the party!"

"We'll see what we can do." Andy said. "Just make sure y'all are *really* feelin' up to it. Wouldn't want to go against doctor's orders."

"Right."

Andy stood and stretched, joints popping.

"Alright, gang. You heard the man. Let's make like a tree and get out of here."

The three said their goodbyes and filed out of the room, Dink closing his eyes as the door closed. Out in the hall, they took a moment of pause. Vick rested against the wall.

"Back to our regularly scheduled programming," he said. "Gods. What a week."

"Chin up. We've still got some planning to do. You guys wanna help make Dink a costume?" Cici asked.

"What would he even be? The Winter Soldier?"

"I've got a pretty funny idea. We'll need to shop for it, though."

"Fine by me," Andy said. "Let's hit up the thrift store."

The group was on their way at that point, heading down the streets toward the business district. They had a few hours until the shops closed up, the perfect amount of time to prep themselves for the weekend.

Vick helped Andy pick out some clothes for the dance, whereas Cici shopped in secret, hiding her items in large paper bags. By the end of the night, the teens parted and went their separate ways. Andy was left alone again, back at his lakeside home.

He trudged up the wooden steps, arms laden with shopping bags. Fumbling for his keys, Andy couldn't help but look off toward the diner in the distance. He thought about Drew again, wondering where he's run off to, if he's even run off at all. For a stint, he thought that maybe he should head up to the place himself. But the fear of Drew's inevitable rejection was stronger.

Andy unlocked the door and stepped inside, putting his bags on the kitchen counter. Otto greeted him with a meow.

Moving toward his room, Andy passed a vaguely familiar photo, one he'd snagged from home before leaving for good.

Him, his father and a strange woman, one with a warm smile.

Of course, Andy knew the identity of the woman—but rather unfortunately, he no longer knew *who* exactly she was.

He had to wonder to himself; once a memory was taken, was it gone forever? Or did it now belong to that entity? And if it belonged to the entity, could Andy ever hope to get it back?

It was a question to ponder at another time. The boy was exhausted, both physically and emotionally. There was a good chance he would sleep for the next few days until the festival.

He turned off his light and laid across his bed. Pulling the covers over himself, Andy got nice and snug, his eyes drifting toward the crescent moon outside.

Though this whole adventure brought up many uncertainties, the sun would still rise in the morning. Things would come around again.

Tomorrow was another day.

Epilogue

Late at night, the crickets chirping, the owls hooting. The main concert was just beginning to wrap up, dozens of couples lining up around the square, scrubbing away their face paint and hastily getting dressed in finer clothes.

Andy scanned the bustling crowd, senses on high alert ever since he arrived at the grounds. There was an overabundance of stimuli. The cold air, the scent of roasted nuts and caramel apples, the voices of hundreds chattering in unison. Strings of twinkling lights cast a multicolored glow upon the many masked revelers.

But where, oh where, was his date? Andy looked and looked for his dance partner, but to no avail. There wasn't any fishing happening in a crowd like this.

That was, until a striking blue blazer caught his eye. Andy turned to see the Vampire sauntering toward him, face obscured by a sequin-encrusted disguise.

"Fancy running into you here," Vick said. "Ready to tear up the dance floor?"

Andy's eye twitched, looking down at his stuffy, thrift-store suit. "This is a lot more formal than I was thinking."

"Getting cold feet?"

"Me?" Andy turned on a false bravado, puffing out his chest. "If I can handle all that adventure junk, I can handle a few slides and steps."

"Just be careful not to step on my toes, Baryshnikov. These shoes are a pain to polish."

The sound of a sultry saxophone navigated its way through the air. Vick grinned as he took Andy's hand and pulled him close.

"Here, follow my lead," he said. Andy blinked. His heart raced. He tried to focus on his steps. Sheesh, he was clumsy.

Still, with Vick's help, he was able to get in a few vaguely elegant moves. A spin, and a dip, and the two were face to face. The world melted away for a brief stint.

But then, as Vick pulled him upright, Andy stumbled, his foot catching on Vick's shoe. He pitched backward, colliding with a tall figure.

"Watch it," a familiar voice snapped. Andy looked up to see Hudson glaring down at him. But that wasn't right, he was supposed to be on the stage. And was this one missing an arm?

"Dink," Andy laughed. "Aw, man. That's really good."

"Thanks," piped Cici, stepping out from behind him. "Largely due to the costume work, I'm sure."

She was accompanied by Tanya, who herself made a rare appearance in a flowy dress.

The whole gang was here. Andy felt warm. How nice to see everyone cutting loose after all that mess. It was moments like this that he cherished, these memories that meant the most.

"Already out of bed," Vick stepped up to Dink. "You sure got better fast. Don't tell me that was all an act."

"Man, he lost an arm." Andy said.

"He could be right," said Dink. "You will never know. I am quite the talented actor."

Vick bobbed his head back and forth. "Yeah, sure. We'll work on your uh…*speech patterns* next week."

"I think it's good enough," Cici giggled. "We could probably get some freebies around town with it. Nobody would suspect a thing."

"Besides Mr. Hudson havin' a head cold, maybe." Andy said.

"Might want to get the arm situation figured out, in that case," said Vick.

"Cici and I on it." Dink said.

"I'm building a prosthesis for him to use," Cici added. "It'll be near-lifelike once it's done."

"So how's that work with the shapeshifting?" Vick asked.

Cici and Dink looked at each other in realization.

Andy shook his head. "Well, I, for one, am glad we can just enjoy the festival together. No nonsense."

As if on cue, the band struck up a lively tune, the brass section blaring, the drums tumbling along. Cici's eye lit up.

"Ooh, I love this song!" she exclaimed, grabbing Dink's hand. "Come on, let's go dance!"

Dink hadn't the time to protest, dragged away into the swarm. Tanya shrugged and followed after them, a coy grin on her face.

Vick turned to Andy, pointing to him dramatically.

"What do you say, Kessler? Ready for round two?"

Andy nodded eagerly, offering his hands.

"Bring it on," he said.

As Vick swept him back into the dance, Andy let the music wash over him. He savored every moment, the coolness of Vick's hands. The worry, the danger, the threat of the unknown, what was it all in the face of this? All that mattered was the here and now, lost in the magic of the night.

"Hey, I was thinking," Vick started. "Maybe in a bit, we can blow this lame dance and go see a movie. I hear Brethren Clown Two dropped Thursday and *nobody's* in the theatre."

"Brethren Clown *Two*," Andy quirked a brow. "I haven't even seen the first one yet."

"I'll get you caught up on the lore," Vick brought Andy back upright, giving him a pat on the arm. "C'mon, let's go before the others notice."

Andy turned back toward the crowd one last time.

He smiled, and followed close behind.

They had a fun night ahead.

The End.

GLOSSARY

The 'world of Hudsonville,' as it were, has quite a few key words, some which may be familiar, some of which may not be. Here is a list of common terms used by the denizens of this world, as well as a few bits of lore you may not have known.

Agartha – A vast, deserted world at the center of the Earth, previously home to the Fae.

Bolter – Large river worms that have been domesticated for use in travel by the citizens of Hudsonville. Their large mouths are capable of scooping up dozens of fish at a time as they slide downstream.

Brethren Clown – A cinematic flop directed by local Hudsonville filmmaker Doug Squawker. It follows two brothers, Arthur and Melvin, who find themselves trying to save their failing family circus. While Melvin attempts to take a more pragmatic approach to the problem, Arthur carves for himself a bizarre life of crime.

Bunyip – Aquatic marsupials native to the flooded regions of Australia, though a small population has since adapted to the pools of Monongahela Valley. Bunyips are notoriously territorial and possess an uncanny ability to sense even the smallest disturbances in the water around them. Their thick, oily fur provides excellent insulation, while their webbed claws make them formidable swimmers.

Carcosan Heirloom – Mysterious artifacts that boast powerful magic at the cost of one's mind and body, the fragmented conscience inside asking for greater and greater sacrifices in order to satiate itself.

Changeling – Grey-skinned natives to Agartha, powered both by sugar and unstable dark magic. Their small, yet incredibly dense bodies are capable of shapeshifting into most any humanoid creature they lay their eyes on—they can even copy the same language of the person whose form they take! Due to common mutations in Changelings, such as extra eyes, limbs or horns, these disguises are not always perfect, and their mutated traits will often carry over no matter what form they take.

Colony worms – Hyper-intelligent worms that cluster together into various forms. Clusters are capable of transforming certain parts of their biology in order to act as organs. Once bound together, colony worms usually do not drift too far apart.

Cryptid – Any species of animal (or in some cases, intelligent humanoid) that has not been widely acknowledged by Human science. While they do not possess any inherent magical traits, they are often considered to be in the same camp as Supernaturals.

Drakes – Like dragons, but small and domesticated. drakes are four-legged reptiles with two leathery wings on their backs. Over the years, they've been kept as pets and livestock by hidden populations around the world. Livestock for what, you might ask? The answer would be their venom, which is commonly used in Supernatural cures and potions.

Elf – Fundamentally linked to the natural world, Elves are a long-lived, wise and durable people who protect the forests of Earth. Their blood, once exposed to the open air, is sappy and like molasses, often hardening into bark-like growths on their skin when wounded. These growths act as an additional layer of protection from the elements, be that blade or beast. As they age, the Elf's body becomes more immobile, until they become fully rooted in the ground, becoming trees.

Fae – A family of Supernatural creatures characterized by their shimmering blood and advanced technology. Includes Changelings, Willow Wisps, Pixies and the like. Most Fae have been driven to extinction by the hands of The Natural Order.

God – Powerful beings that are directly descended from the Outer Gods. Unlike the truly immortal Outer Gods, lesser Gods are sustained by the worship of mortals. Amidst the pantheon of lesser Gods are the God of Humanity, Hastur, the Goddess of the Woods, Shub, the God of Destruction, Cthulhu and the God of Death, Tereshek.

Gorgon – People on top; snakes on the bottom. Gorgons (or Lamia, depending on the region) are distinct for their humanoid upper halves connecting to large snake-like tails. They often sport a pair of glasses as a protective measure, as their stare is known to cause paralysis in others.

Grim – A race of undead people whose souls are trapped within their withering bodies. Through a healthy mix of preservatives and magic, they are able to get by relatively unbothered in life. When in a pinch, they can draw on the power of their patron God, Zushak, to telekinetically manipulate the physical world.

Hudsonville – One of many hidden Supernatural settlements, stationed in the heart of the Appalachian Mountains. Hudsonville has been governed by its namesake, Solomon J. Hudson, for the last 35 years. Its citizens enjoy relative peace at the cost of their freedom, unable to go beyond the confines of Monongahela Valley without getting into trouble.

Despite the existential nature of it all, the city is still quite pleasant, connected through branching rivers, waterways, sidewalks and bridges. Aesthetically, it mirrors something of a small American town, albeit much more walkable and compact, as well as with its fair share of expectantly fantastical structures.

It has all of what you would expect from a self-sufficient civilization—its own power grid, public access television, radio, restaurants and bars, a library, a school, you name it. There's a good variety to the neighborhoods as well, ranging from traditional apartment complexes and townhomes to stranger fixtures like underground burrows and hives.

The local economy runs on trading, favors and, most notably, a pseudo-currency called Jold, which can be exchanged at a number of businesses run by the troublesome Djinni, Gene.

Human – The most abundant intelligent life on Earth, Humans are rather unremarkable in comparison to their Supernatural peers—however, this power indifference did little to stop the Human spirit and its will to come out on top. Against all odds, Humans managed to overwhelm the deific forces which control this world through their numbers and their wits. Most Humans in the modern era live in complete ignorance of the Supernatural; the few who do live in abject fear.

Kloon – An invasive species to the surface world, kloons are small, rat-like creatures without a mind or a soul of their own. They have faces like sharp-toothed clowns, often sporting party-hat-like protrusions on their heads. Their bodies are small and fuzzy, and should you find yourself dissecting one, you would find that its innards are wholly made up of wrapped candies. Feeding on strong negative emotions, kloons are seasonal creatures, and only emerge to wreak havoc once every 27 months.

Kloonpile – Matured kloons that have grown exponentially in size. They often sport multiple tumorous growths that will eventually birth more kloons.

Kobold – Small, lizard-like people who are native to the volcanic regions of Earth. Their scales are highly resistant to heat. In Kobold culture, cuisine is king; they often have large scale competitive cook-offs for status and bragging rights. Famous among the Kobolds is Geb Fizetti, a native of Hudsonville who runs his own diner, Yellow Devil's Dive.

Magic – There are many kinds of magic, all operating on the clause of give and take. While most effects of utilizing magic are negligible, overuse and overexertion can bring physical and mental harm to its user.
Most magic is performed by making a pact with a God. Some of these pacts, such as with Vampires, are automatically processed with the birth of the creature. Other pacts require a bit more commitment.
There are five subsects of magic that are widely known; in many cases, these subsects will overlap with one another in order to create an array of spells and incantations.
Cosmic – The most powerful magic, its abilities not limited by the laws of any reality. It is impossible to fully comprehend the

extent of its uses, as mortals are only capable of mastering its most basic elements: destruction, creation and control.

Psychic – Dictates the mind and soul, covering all sense of self and conscious; mind reading, mind control, the like.

Dark – Covers most illusory magic and abilities that alter perception. Think invisibility and unnatural darkness.

Alchemy – Transmutation, converting one element to another. Due to its approachable, scientific nature, it is widely regarded to be the easiest form of magic to learn for those who are not naturally gifted.

Elemental – Self-explanatory, dealing with the elements, such as ice, fire and electricity.

Minotaur – A hearty people with the heads of bulls and the bodies of Humans. They are believed to be distant relatives to Werewolves, though their exact connection is uncertain. Like their lycanthropic cousins, most Minotaurs possess brute strength and durable hides, with horns to boot.

Mycarnid – Mushroom-like denizens of Mycopolis. Mycarnids are made up of a sentient, fleshy fungus that gathers the bones of dead creatures in order to make up their own skeletons. They are covered in sensory organs, and are slowly evolving to be indistinguishable from Humans. This is theorized to take a few more centuries at most. While not quite considered intelligent life, Mycarnids are capable of speech and a limited range of emotions. They appear to have their own form of society as well—it brings a number of ethical questions to mind.

Mycopolis – A city of Mycarnids just beneath the surface of Monongahela Valley. Its architecture is, of course, made entirely of giant, carved-out mushrooms. The Mycarnids there have learned from Drew Warren to mimic the societal structure of the surface world, complete with their own primitive cafes, maps and nurseries for their fungal young.

Onierovore – Natives to Onira, or The Dreamlands as they are more commonly known, Onierovores are dark creatures that devour the dreams of mortals; as part of their digestive process, Onierovores recycle the excess psychic energy created by dreams, funneling it back into the cosmos for others to draw from. Most prefer their presence to go unknown…

Outer Gods – Beings that are direct extensions of the primordial chaos, Azethoth. The Outer Gods hold dominion over entire realities, their most primal task being that of keeping the chaos 'entertained.' As far as this universe is concerned, its ruling Outer God is that of the storyteller, Nyarlathotep.

Pelé the Clown – A not-so-popular Canadian children's cartoon character. Pelé is a circus clown whose merry band travels across realities seeking adventure. The disastrous physical release saw thousands of its copies being buried in the mountains of Appalachia, after catastrophically poor sales pushed its production company, Switch Studios, to bankruptcy. Funnily enough, Pelé's titular series has managed to garner a rich cult following among a scant few citizens of Hudsonville.

Raiders – Pirates of the post-apocalyptic wasteland, raiders use whatever scrap they can muster to make everyone else's lives miserable. They love the smell of diesel.

Rangers – Hudsonville's police force; worshippers of Shub, they are dedicated to maintaining the secrecy of Monongahela Valley and its residents, through any means necessary. Their group is currently led by two Elders, Balrog and Fia, and one Grandmaster, Goggen Longstrider. Ranger Scouts are recruited at a young age and sworn in through a magic oath of silence. Through this pact, they are given the gifts of chloromancy, or plant magic.

It is only when a Ranger is promoted to Scoutmaster that they earn the right to their own voice. By then, most seldom use it.

Sandworm – Believed to be distant relatives of bolters, sandworms are enormous creatures native to Agartha. They rely on vibrations in the ground above in order to find their prey, and use their shovel-shaped faces to quickly burrow through the earth at high speeds. They grew to their current size from an overabundance of fairy dust, itself a result of the 1857 Fae massacre.

Supernatural (proper noun) – Any entity, be it man or animal, that possesses innate magical attributes, i.e. Vampires, Werewolves, Changelings, etc. Sometimes used as a blanket term to cover all manner of both Supernatural creatures and Cryptids, though Cryptids are technically a classification of their own.

"Tep's sake!" – Shorthand; "for Nyarlathotep's sake" doesn't exactly roll off the tongue.

The Natural Order – A Human organization of self-proclaimed 'monster hunters.' They are incredibly traditional, sporting medieval armor and weapons and often foregoing modern amenities. They are worshippers of the god of destruction, Cthulhu, and see the Supernatural as an unnatural plague that threatens to replace the Human race. Currently at the helm of The Natural Order stands the proud Prince Kopernicus III.

Werewolf – Shapeshifters born of a viral curse, one which causes them to transform into monstrous, fuzzy forms under the light of the full moon...as well as under any intense bouts of emotion. The two alter egos that make up for a Werewolf generally contrast one another a great deal, their personalities often butting heads; however, deep down, you can still find the core of the person hidden within the confines of their savage minds.

Vampire – Gifted in magic from birth and somewhat susceptible to sunburns, Vampires are often regarded as the most powerful race of Supernaturals on the planet. They can live for hundreds, if not thousands of years, and many powerful bloodlines from decades ago still rule over their ancient kingdoms with an iron fist.

Xita – Single-eyed, bug-like humanoids that are believed to be descended from the stars. Their chitin is tough and durable, and they can withstand great amounts of pressure without breaking. Male Xita are born with wings, whereas the females are born with an extra pair of arms. Xita are very work-focused and are naturally inclined to perform arduous tasks for the benefit of their communities.